BLOOD
MOON
RISING

ALSO BY MARK DAWSON

MARK **DAWSON**
BLOOD MOON RISING

A BEATRIX ROSE THRILLER

THOMAS & MERCER

Published by Thomas & Mercer, Seattle

www.apub.com

Amazon, the Amazon logo, and Thomas & Mercer are trademarks of Amazon.com, Inc., or its affiliates.

ISBN-13: 978-1503944381
ISBN-10: 1503944387

Cover design by Lisa Horton

Printed in the United States of America

To Mrs D, FD and SD

Chapter One

It was three in the morning when Beatrix Rose finally reached the Wiltshire village where Lydia Chisholm made her home. She had been following her for two hours, all the way south from London. She turned the stolen Kawasaki off the A road, passed a cute village pub and then turned sharply behind it and followed a gentle rise to a series of even prettier houses. Beatrix had extinguished the headlamp five minutes earlier, and now she killed the engine and freewheeled to a stop. She flicked out the kickstand and rested the bike on it carefully. Chisholm's top-of-the-range BMW drove on and parked next to a dark blue Audi A3. Beatrix jogged along the road, keeping close to the thick verge of hawthorn, her rucksack bouncing up and down on her back.

Chisholm and her husband got out, locked the door and climbed the steps from the road to the front door. Chisholm went first, opening the door and stepping inside. Her husband followed. A hall light flicked on.

Beatrix edged closer to the house. Some of the nearby dwellings were thatched, and all of them looked expensive. The mainline station was a ten-minute drive away, and London was ninety minutes by train from there. It was at the edge of a reasonable distance to consider commuting, and Beatrix guessed that the people who did travel in from the village were more likely to be senior staff who had the latitude to work from home. That supposition was borne out by the cars that were parked along the edge of the road: Range Rovers, Porsches, Jaguars, more BMWs. The houses had big extensions, manicured gardens, swimming pools. There was money here, and influence, too. But she had known that already.

Chisholm and her husband had been in town all day. Chisholm had been to a meeting of the board of the private security contractors that she had established after leaving Group Fifteen. Manage Risk was a serious concern, with offices around the world, and it counted among its senior employees one of Chisholm's old colleagues in the Group, Joshua Joyce. Beatrix had been in Somalia last week where she had reacquainted herself with Joyce. He had been assigned as security on a freighter that had been captured by al-Shabaab off the coast. Beatrix had infiltrated the country and the town in which the terrorists had made their stronghold.

Joyce was an ex-employee now.

She had struck his name from her Kill List.

Beatrix had returned home to Morocco to find excellent news waiting for her. Michael Pope, the new Control of Group Fifteen, had reported that they had located Chisholm, too. Beatrix had immediately boarded a flight from Marrakech to Heathrow. She had followed Chisholm for two days and constructed the plan that was now drawing to its conclusion.

Chisholm's house was a large square building with broad windows on both sides of the porch, five windows on the first floor and two dormers on top. It looked as if it was in the middle of a refurbishment program. The stonework had been repointed, and the lime render on the exterior walls was fresh. There was an alarm box beneath the eaves and a satellite dish positioned discreetly away from public view. There was a broad lawn to the right of the house with what looked like a tennis court behind it and an ornamental garden to the left. The land sloped up steeply behind the property, with the deeper darkness of a copse of tall fir and oak providing a border to that side.

Beatrix waited until the downstairs light was switched off and then moved forward. A stone wall separated the property from the road, and she slipped between it and the BMW, dropped down to her belly and slithered forward. The car was still warm, the engine ticking as the temperature bled away in the coolness of the night. She removed the rucksack and opened it, took out three pounds of Semtex and a disposable mobile phone that she had purchased earlier that day. The phone was wrapped around the detonator with gaffer tape, and that, in turn, was wrapped around the plastique. She took the wire that ran from the phone and connected it to the detonator, peeled away the adhesive backing and pressed the bomb to the underside of the car, right below the fuel tank.

She had a few hours to wait.

She made her way back to her motorbike and hid it in a nearby lane, beneath a railway bridge that boomed and shook as a late night goods train rumbled over it. She clambered over a nearby fence and negotiated a paddock and then a pig field until she had found her way to the large garden at the back of Chisholm's house. There was a tumbledown shed next to the vegetable patch, and it offered a decent view of the house, the BMW and the road for twenty yards on either side. It was perfect.

Beatrix took out her night vision binoculars, zipped up her leather jacket and settled down to wait.

———

It was dawn when the early commuters made their way out of their houses to their cars. There had been no movement outside the house until then. The upstairs bathroom light had flicked on at three, and then, five minutes later, it had been extinguished again. Someone using the bathroom and then going back to bed. There had been nothing else to concern her since then.

She had taken the opportunity to study the rest of the property: there was a large extension to the rear, a kitchen that she could see when she focussed her binoculars on the ground floor window that faced her, an oil tank fifty feet away from her hiding position. It was a desirable property. Expensive.

There had been no question of sleep for her. She was too keyed up for that, and far too professional to allow even the slightest possibility that she might be distracted and miss something important. Her eyes stung a little as the sun cast a thin glow over the top of the ridge that formed the slope on the other side of the valley, but she would have no rest now. That would come later.

A car rolled slowly down the hill towards the main road.

It was six-thirty.

Just a commuter. She let it go.

The lights in the kitchen came on.

Beatrix raised her binoculars. She caught a glimpse of a woman from behind: a cream shirt, a black skirt, a jacket held in the crook of one arm. The woman moved in and out of sight until she paused at the window and looked out, and Beatrix confirmed her target.

Hello, Lydia.

Beatrix had to wait just another ten minutes before she came out of the front of the house, a slice of half-eaten toast in one hand and a travel beaker in the other. She negotiated the steps to the road, acknowledged a jogger who was running with her dog, rested the beaker on the roof of the car as she opened the door, took the beaker again and got inside.

Beatrix unzipped her leather jacket and took out her phone.

She had two numbers to call.

She selected the first and let it ring.

"Hello?"

"Hello, Lydia."

"Who is this?"

"I'd be surprised if you've forgotten."

"I don't . . ."

"It's Number One."

Lydia's voice was horribly unfamiliar. The last time they had met, Beatrix had stabbed her in the throat with a letter opener, and the blade had pierced her larynx. Pope had explained that it had been necessary to perform an emergency laryngectomy in order to save her life. A speech valve had been fitted to enable her to speak. Her words sounded wet and awkward, and they were difficult to interpret.

"Where are you?"

"Looking right at you."

She watched as Chisholm yanked her head around, trying to spot her.

Panicking.

That was good.

She was right to panic.

"I'm here," Beatrix said. "I can see you very well. You're in your car. You've just finished your breakfast. Toast and coffee to go."

Chisholm kept looking, unable to find her.

"What do you want?"

"What do you think I want?"

"To talk? We can talk. Come into the house. We can talk about whatever you want."

"I don't think so."

The car door started to open.

"Don't do that," Beatrix warned. "Stay in the car."

"Come on," she said, looking round again. "This is crazy. I'm coming out. We can talk . . ."

"There's a bomb under your car, Lydia."

She stopped moving.

"A pound of Semtex. Right underneath you."

The door closed again. Chisholm was still, looking through the windscreen, dead ahead. "What do you want?"

"The last ten years of my life back. My husband. To see my little girl grow up. But you can't help me with any of that."

"I'm sorry," Lydia said. "Control gave us a direct order. I know you have a reason to be angry, but you should take it up with him."

"I intend to," she said. "I'm working my way up. But you're next."

Beatrix came out of the shed and negotiated the garden, following the boundary fence for the next property until she had a better view of the BMW and the front of the house.

"Let me help you," Chisholm offered.

"Okay. Where's Control?"

"I don't know. I swear I don't."

Another car rolled slowly down the road. "Let it go," Beatrix warned.

She did. It disappeared out of sight.

"Come on," Chisholm protested.

"What about the others?"

"Spenser is dead."

"I know. I killed him."

"In Russia. You and John Milton, right?"

"That's right. I knelt down next to him, and I slit his throat from ear to ear."

"And Joyce, too. The thing in Somalia."

"I'm doing well, aren't I? Two down. Four to go."

"I can give you Duffy."

"I'm listening."

"What's that worth to you? You'll leave?"

"Maybe I won't kill your husband."

"Rose . . ."

"Joyce told me Duffy was in Iraq."

"Yes. He is. He works for us. Manage Risk has a contract with American Petroleum. We run security for their executive team. He's been out there for months. I can give you a precise location."

"That's alright. I can take it from here."

"So you'll leave?"

"What do you think? After what you did? Of course not."

"After what *I* did? Come on, Beatrix. Listen to my voice. Listen to what you did to me. I sound like a freak. Isn't that enough?"

"No. Not nearly. Any last words?" She almost laughed. "I'm sorry. That was insensitive of me."

Chisholm slumped back into the seat. Beatrix almost thought she could see the fight drain out of her. She turned her head to the left and looked up the steps to the front of the house. Beatrix looked in that direction and saw that the front door had opened. A man was standing there. Middle-aged, salmon-pink trousers, blazer. Ex-army. Officer class. She paused for a moment, her resolution wavering just a little, and then she remembered, back to a life that seemed a hundred years ago: Lydia Chisholm in Beatrix's front room, her husband and daughter on the sofa, fear and confusion on both of their faces. The unsaid agreement that she and Lucas had shared, the shot from Chisholm's pistol that had killed him, the second shot into Beatrix's shoulder, the terror on Isabella's face and then the black well of sadness and loss that she had willingly thrown herself into so that she might save her daughter's life.

Beatrix remembered all of that as she thumbed through the phone for the second number that she needed.

"Beatrix," Chisholm begged. "Please."

"Your husband. Robert Chisholm. Royal Anglians, First Battalion. Set up Manage Risk's London office with you. Shall I take him out, too?"

"No. He has nothing to do with any of this."

"Hypocrite."

"Rose . . ."

"Goodbye."

Beatrix called the number. The BMW remained intact for a fraction of a second, raised up off the ground by the unfolding viciousness of the detonation beneath it, but an instant later the fuel tank ruptured and it was consumed by a terrific blast. The quicksilver expansion of the hot gasses from the explosive created a pressure wave that would have crushed Lydia before the tank burst, but immolated fragments of her body and the car were thrown for hundreds of yards in all directions. The boom echoed around the village and out into the valley beyond, bouncing off the slopes of the ridge and echoing back again like a peal of distant thunder. Every window in the Chisholms' house and the houses nearby shattered. There was a terrific tumult for a moment, and then all fell silent. The peace did not last: the pigs in the pig field started to squeal in panic, the horses in the paddock whinnied and bucked, and there was a loud wail from the house as an alarm sounded.

Beatrix felt numbed. She didn't feel any sense of triumph nor even satisfaction, but then she hadn't expected to, either.

Three down.

Three to go.

Chapter Two

Captain Michael Pope, newly appointed as Control, had arranged for an agent to work as a barista in the Covent Garden branch of Starbucks. It was simple tradecraft and yet as effective today as when Somerset Maugham had met his old butter-woman in a Geneva marketplace. Beatrix had palmed her a note after receiving her latte and had received a reply in the same fashion when she dropped in for a coffee the following day.

Pope would meet her at Gatwick.

He was waiting for her in the seats arranged across the large hall that preceded security. She bought a coffee and watched for a moment to check that he was not observed. Beatrix had no history with Pope, and so she had to be careful. He had been cooperative so far, but then he had little choice. She had evidence that would cause significant damage to the government if it were ever released. Pope's predecessor was a very bad man, and he had been using Group Fifteen and its cadre of assassins as his own personal hit squad for years. That kind of information would be very destructive if it ever got out into the world.

She had to tread lightly. Pope seemed like a good man, but she was not naïve enough to think that he was immune from manipulation by the mandarins who pulled the strings above him.

He was reading a copy of the *Telegraph*, the large broadsheet spread wide and obscuring his face, and as she approached, Beatrix could not help but notice that the front-page story below the fold recounted the unexplained murder of a security analyst outside her Wiltshire house.

"You've made more noise than I expected," Pope said as she took the seat next to him.

"I wasn't in a particularly subtle mood."

The pain had flared up as she drove south to the airport, and she had already taken as much morphine as she felt comfortable taking. Pope still did not know about her diagnosis. The only other person who knew, other than Mohammed, her housekeeper in Marrakech, was John Milton, and there was something about his stolid dependability that said he would keep her secret.

"I might have what you need to go after Duffy," he said.

She felt the familiar tightening in her stomach as she sipped her coffee and waited for him to continue.

"We need to discuss it first. I've given you Joyce and Chisholm. No questions asked."

"What do you want, Pope?"

"There needs to be a little *quid pro quo* with this one. You scratch my back . . . you know how it is. The intelligence . . . well, it's very sensitive, and I was only able to get it by promising that we would help iron out a few problems that Manage Risk and Duffy have helped to cause."

"Whose problems?"

"The government's."

"That sounds like you're making this conditional," she said.

"No . . ."

"And I thought we agreed that this was going to be unconditional."

"It is. By and large, anyway. You don't *have* to do it this way."

She nodded. "I could do it myself."

"You could. They know that. And they know you could release the evidence on Control. Don't think they've underestimated the trouble that would cause, because they haven't."

"So what do *they* want?"

"A bit of history first." He took out a folded printout from his pocket. It was a map. "You know where he is. Joyce told you, didn't he?"

"Iraq. Chisholm confirmed it. But I don't know where."

"There's an enormous oilfield at Rumaila. The biggest in the country and they think the third largest in the world. The Iraqis say there could be eighteen billion barrels. It's worth a ridiculous amount. The oil ministry auctioned the contract off six months ago, and they had Exxon and Mobil bidding on the one hand and a consortium of BP and the Chinese on the other. The Americans won, which didn't make the government particularly happy, as you can imagine. The treasury revenue on this is enormous. And frankly, we could do with the money."

"What does this have to do with Duffy?"

"I'm getting to that. It goes without saying the area isn't safe. The Americans lost three executives when they went down to spec it out. The insurgents didn't take too kindly to them and had them shot. So the companies invested in better security. Our friends, Manage Risk, tendered and won the contract. They've been supplying ex-Spec Op guys, SAS, SEALs and Rangers, and they've kept a lid on things for the most part." He stabbed a finger on the map. "Rumaila. Twenty miles from the Kuwaiti border, just south of Basra. Sunni territory. It was discovered in 1953 by the Basra Petroleum Company, but then it was confiscated by the Iraqi government. The Sunnis have always maintained a claim to it."

"This is very interesting, Pope, but I don't have time for history. Just tell me where Duffy is and what you want me to do."

He ignored her and continued. "The locals have been protesting ever since the Americans won the contract. They've picketed the offices, targeted the officials and vandalised the drill sites. It came to a head last week. There was a big protest, several thousand locals, and it started to turn ugly. They tried to break into the compound. There were a few Iraqi soldiers there, but mostly it was men from Manage Risk. They opened fire on the crowd with machine guns. Two hundred injured, sixteen dead. It's been a very big deal down there. The locals tried to get the men prosecuted, but the charges were all thrown out."

"I read about it. Unreliable evidence."

"And it was. The judge said it was built on testimony given in exchange for immunity. The reason you should be interested in this is because Bryan Duffy was one of the five defendants. He was Manage Risk's top man on the ground that day. The evidence suggests he gave the order to fire."

"He's still there?"

Pope nodded. "Working between Basra and the oil field. One of the other defendants is having a crisis of conscience. His name is Mackenzie West. He's a man of faith and he can't square what happened with there being no punishment. We've heard through channels that he's ready to give evidence against the other four. Manage Risk knows that. They've trumped up a bogus medical reason why he needs to be taken out of circulation. We need you to go and get him out."

"What's it got to do with us?"

"If the case against Manage Risk is successful, it will make it very hard for the Americans to hold on to the oilfield. There's already been a backlash, and if this can be made to stick, it'll get much, much worse. BP has been told by the Iraqis that there's a good chance that the contract will be torn up and the field put out to tender again. The government is anxious that should happen. All this intel is coming from MI6. Everyone wins: you get Duffy, the Iraqis get justice, BP gets the oilfield, the treasury gets billions in fresh taxes."

"Very neat. He's protected?"

"By the best they've got."

"How many?"

"There's three hundred in Basra. Good men, not chumps."

"So it wouldn't be easy?"

"No. Certainly not."

"And I don't have a choice?"

"No, of course you do. You could go in yourself and take Duffy out."

"But I'll get no cooperation?"

"I won't be able to help if you do that. My hands are tied. If you help, I'm authorised to get you into the country and arm you. If you don't, I can't. And they want you to remember that you still have Connor English and Control that you need to find. And they're looking for them for you now."

She snorted dismissively. "They've been looking for a year, and there's been nothing."

"They'll still find them faster than you will."

"So I could work with you or do it myself. There's another option. I could release the information I have."

"They're hoping you won't think it's necessary to do that. The loose partnership we've had so far has worked well for you. There's no reason why it has to stop working now."

She shook her head. She was tempted to ignore him and go it alone, but that would take much longer, and if there was one thing she did not have, it was time.

"Tell them I'll do it," she said.

Chapter Three

Beatrix flew British Airways to Marrakech. She was tired and in pain, but she had arranged a meeting with a particular contact who was difficult to pin down, and the only day he was available was today. She had placed a large order that was going to make him a lot of money. She was sure that he would be glad that he had made the time in his day to see her.

She had little in the way of luggage, just a carry-on bag with a few things inside it, and so at least she was reasonably unencumbered as she stepped into the car at the taxi rank and asked for the carpet shop that Abdullah used to front his other business.

The traffic was heavy, but the driver, mercifully, was silent. Beatrix was able to spend the time collecting her thoughts. She had made good progress. Oliver Spenser had been eliminated in Russia when she came to Milton's aid. Joyce had been more difficult to reach in Somalia, but she had managed it. Chisholm had just been a case of good intelligence. She had been the easiest of the three. She had adopted another name, but she was still in the country, tangled up in the spider's web of intercepts that ended at GCHQ, and it had been a matter of time before the signals were decoded and she was tracked down.

Three names had been scrubbed from her list.

Bryan Duffy would be more difficult. She had not been to Iraq for many years, but she knew very well how infiltrating a lawless state could present particular challenges. If Manage Risk was the same as the American security firms that had rushed in to gorge on the carcass of Saddam's old regime, it would be the equivalent of a small and supremely well-equipped army in a country that was ill-equipped to stand up to them.

This would be the most difficult target so far.

The taxi stopped in a quiet side road. The shop catered to the tourist trade, touting rolls of carpet and Berber rugs for extortionate prices. Beatrix told the driver to wait and went into the shop through the back entrance. Abdullah was drinking mint tea in a large wicker chair. He was old, fat and lecherous, and Beatrix found him repulsive, but he had contacts and discretion, and that was enough for her to put up with him.

"Beatrix! My dear girl."

"Abdullah."

"How are you?"

"Tolerable." She had no inclination to engage in small talk with him. "Did you get what I wanted?"

"You are fortunate, Beatrix. It wasn't easy."

"Did you get them?"

"Yes, I did."

"Everything?"

"Yes."

"Good. I need you to deliver it."

He looked at her gravely. "It is not going to be cheap."

"How much?"

Abdullah named a price.

It was very, very expensive, and Beatrix knew that he would be adding a fifty or sixty per cent markup to the price he was paying God knows who to source the order for him. That was the cost of doing business with this type of merchant and this type of merchandise. Same the world over. Not much she could do about it.

"I'll transfer half tonight," she said. "Half on receipt."

"That is acceptable."

"When can you deliver?"

"Tomorrow morning. Are you in the same place?"

"Yes."

"Then they will come to you hidden in crates of fruit. I hope you like orange juice."

"Can't beat it," she said.

Chapter Four

There is a series of buildings on the bank of the Thames, some on the water and some set back from it. They are anonymous and bland, and for all intents and purposes, they accommodate a host of companies and organisations that look like all the other companies in all the other similar buildings in the area. The real purposes of those companies are jealously guarded, cloaked with the draconian protection of the Official Secrets Act and unknown to the thousands of ordinary Londoners who pass them every day. There is the hulking mass of the building constructed to look like a Mesopotamian pyramid. It could hardly be less conspicuous and is referred to by the locals as Babylon-on-Thames. Its brashness was a design choice. The government's decision in the middle of the last decade to acknowledge that it was the headquarters of the Secret Intelligence Service gave an official imprimatur to a fact that was well known in any event. The building's ostentatiousness also has the useful side effect of attracting attention to it and deflecting curiosity away from some of the other buildings in the immediate neighbourhood.

In that sense, it is a lightning rod.

Those buildings, and the clandestine organisations that work within them, would have been *much* more interesting to those with even a passing interest in national security.

There is one building, for example, that is particularly anonymous. It is separated from the MI6 building by two lanes of busy traffic and is hidden down a narrow side street that can trace its history all the way back to the Great Fire. The neighbouring buildings are old and historically significant, but this one, erected on the site of a Luftwaffe bomb, is a banal sixties infill. There is no reason to give it a second glance. The brass plaque on the wall and the notice above the desk in the utilitarian reception advertise "Global Logistics." A search of the internet furnishes the information that the company was founded twenty-five years earlier, is engaged in the import and export business, and has a board of directors who are as bland and uninteresting as the architecture of the building in which they work.

None of that is true.

It is the headquarters of Group Fifteen, a beyond top-secret, quasi-military organisation that is responsible for implementing the foreign policy of the United Kingdom when diplomacy and the more nuanced methods of the Secret Intelligence Service have failed. It is responsible, for example, for the liquidation and elimination of enemies of the state or those men and women who, for whatever reason, stand between Her Majesty's Government and the pursuit of its global ambitions.

Captain Michael Pope, the new Control of Group Fifteen, parked his unremarkable Audi Q5 in the underground garage and stepped out. He was unremarkable himself: black hair, a rugged face, the build and bearing of a military man. He walked to the secure elevator, activated it with his thumbprint, faced the unblinking eye of the security camera so that his identity could be verified and then waited for it to carry him to his office.

The office floor was divided into cubicles, and it hummed with quiet industry. The staff were seconded from the internal and external security agencies, with others assigned from the Ministry of Defence. They monitored ongoing operations, vetted potential new recruits, researched targets and provided intelligence to agents in the field. Pope had benefitted from their professionalism when he had been on operation himself, and he still found it a little jarring to have been promoted into a position where he was responsible for them, rather than the other way around.

He crossed the floor and returned the greetings of the analysts who looked up from their work.

His office was on the side of the building that faced the water, and it boasted a spectacular view over the river and the skyline beyond.

Pope opened the door and went inside.

Sir Benjamin Stone, the Chief of the Secret Intelligence Service, which was more commonly known as MI6, was waiting for him.

"Oh," he said. "Good afternoon, sir. I wasn't expecting you."

"I know," said Stone. He was in his late fifties, a little overweight, and dressed with the stuffy good taste that marked out the better shops on Savile Row. He was sitting on the sofa next to the fireplace. His legs were crossed, and he had a copy of the *Telegraph* spread out across his lap.

"How can I help you?" Pope said breezily as he turned away and took off his coat.

Stone folded the paper and shoved it into the case at his feet. "I wanted to know first-hand how it's going."

"With Rose?"

"Who else."

Pope hung the coat and turned back to Stone. "I saw her yesterday."

"And?"

"She'll do it. Just as you asked."

"Excellent," Stone said. "Well done."

Pope walked across the office to the fireplace. "I wish there was no need to bargain with her like this," he said. "After what she's been through? What Control and the others did? We should be doing everything we can to help her, not putting distractions in her way."

"And we *are* helping her, Pope. We gave her Joshua Joyce in Somalia. That took some fancy footwork. The Americans were not pleased."

"The hostages would all have been dead if it wasn't for her. The SEALs had given up."

"That might be true, but they don't like being blindsided. And they had *no* idea."

Pope ignored that. "Let's be honest about this, sir. We're only helping her with Duffy because it is in our best interests and because she's agreed to do our dirty work for us. She's engaged in SIS work and she's not a serving agent, sir. That makes me very uncomfortable."

"And it's for the best that she isn't an agent. Those oilfields are a very big prize. Billion-pound assets. Washington is heavily invested in them."

That was true, but it didn't make it right, and Pope suppressed a sigh of impatience. "We're not helping her enough. She'll need backup in Iraq."

"And I told you, we can't be seen to be involved."

"There are ways around that . . ."

Stone held up a hand impatiently. "Your concerns have already been noted, Control. Let's not rehash old ground again. It's tedious. We give her the minimum amount needed. Twelve has no active record. No one knows who he is. He's completely deniable. If he gets caught, then we have no idea who he is or what he's doing there. If Rose gets caught, then we say she was going after Bryan Duffy and it has nothing to do with us. It's perfect. You, though, are different. You *are* known. If you got caught, if the State Department found out who you are and why you were there, trying to interfere with American contracts, the result would be very unpleasant. That's a full-blown diplomatic incident, and I guarantee you we would be completely and utterly buggered. So let me be as clear about this as I can be. I don't want there to be any ambiguity. You are not, repeat *not*, to be involved in any meaningful, practical capacity. You are not to be on the ground. I don't even want you dreaming about Basra. Understand?"

"Yes, sir."

"I mean it, Control."

"I understand."

"And she's a big girl. I'm sure she can sort herself out."

Pope gritted his teeth. "Yes, sir." He went around to the other side of his desk and sat down.

"What about Chisholm?" Stone asked.

"There's not much left of her. Beatrix paid her a visit. Followed her home last night, camped out and then took care of it this morning."

"How?"

"Left a bomb under her car."

"Not quite as . . . visceral as the other two."

"I don't think she cares how they go, sir. She's not into causing them suffering. She isn't a sadist. The way she sees it, they've done her wrong, and now they have to pay. It's like a ledger. An eye for an eye. Simple accounting."

"The police?"

"They're investigating. They won't find anything. Rose is an expert. It's clean."

"Spenser, Joyce and Chisholm. That's three left."

"I'm assuming we still don't know where Connor English and Control are hiding?"

"With Manage Risk. That's obvious. But the company has powerful friends, and they are being protected, Control especially. He could be anywhere in the world. She might need to find him herself."

"She will," Pope said.

He was certain about that.

Chapter Five

She opened the door with the sign that said "La Villa des Orangers" just after eight o'clock. The medina was noisy and clamorous, but when she closed the oak door behind her, it was as if she had been transported into a peaceful idyll. Here, instead of raised voices and the angry horns of cars and vans, she could hear the tinkling of water into the fountain and the sound of meat sizzling on a grill. She dropped her bag and slumped into one of the chairs that overlooked the pool. She let her head hang back and looked up. Her home here was a riad, a traditional Moroccan house with an interior garden. The four walls of the structure made a square of the darkening sky, now shot through with a dozen different colours in the dying sun's last grand gesture. The stone retained the cool, and she closed her eyes and was almost on the point of sleep when she felt eyes upon her.

"Mummy."

She opened her eyes. Her thirteen-year-old daughter, Isabella, was standing between her and the pool.

"Hello, sweetheart. How are you?"

"I'm fine, Mummy. You look tired."

"I am."

"Did you do it?"

"Yes. I did it."

"How?"

"With a bomb."

The girl slipped off her sandals and sat down by her side, dipping her dusty feet in the cool blue water.

"Good. Did you speak to her?"

"Yes."

"So she knew it was you?"

"She did."

"Good."

"I know where the next one is, too. He's in Iraq."

"When are you going?"

"Soon. Two days."

"You can't stay longer?"

"I wish I could, but the information won't be good forever, and he probably knows I'm coming now. The longer I wait, the more time he'll have to prepare. That will mean it is more dangerous."

"I understand, Mummy. It's just . . ."

"I know. But once this is done, we'll be safe. And we can be together all the time."

They sat quietly for a moment. The only sounds were the music of the fountain and her feet splashing in the water.

"I've been practising," she said. "Five hours every day. Ask Mohammed."

"I believe you."

"He says I'm getting better and better."

"That's good, sweetheart. I have something for you. Something else for you to try."

"What is it?"

"It's a surprise. It's being delivered tomorrow."

———————

Isabella went to bed, and Beatrix was about to follow her example when Mohammed came out of the kitchen with a silver salver on which rested a teapot and two clear glasses. He set the tray on the table and hugged her.

"How was it?"

"It's done."

"You look troubled," he said.

"It's nothing."

"Perhaps a glass of tea will help."

She smiled and nodded that perhaps it would. Mohammed was rightly proud of his grandmother's recipe for mint tea. He stripped leaves from the spearmint plant in the courtyard every morning, added a handful to boiling water, sugar and a good tablespoon of gunpowder green tea. He took the glasses and poured the tea from a height so that a thin layer of foam settled on the top.

"Thank you," she said.

Mohammed was the nearest person she had to a friend in the world. They had worked together on an assignment ten years earlier when she was Number Two and he was a corporal in the Moroccan Royal Guard. They had taken out an al Qaeda cell that had been planning a car bombing in the capital, and in the vicious firefight that had followed, she had saved his life. He had helped her buy the riad, and when she said that she was looking for someone to look after the place, Mohammed and his wife had volunteered. Men didn't come more honest and trustworthy, and she was grateful every day that he had agreed to help her.

"You know I would never want to intrude, Miss Beatrix, but I think you should consider telling her."

"Is it obvious?"

"It is obvious that you are unwell. Beyond that? No, it is not obvious. But she is not a stupid girl."

She would have been irritated to have been told what she should or should not do by almost anyone else, but there was something so calming and inherently good about Mohammed that she didn't mind.

"I know," she admitted. "I know I should, but it's difficult. What do I say? How do I say it? She's only just got me back again, and then to go and tell her . . . I don't know, Mohammed. It's going to be difficult. Very difficult."

"That I do not doubt."

They sat in silence for five minutes. She sipped her tea and enjoyed the cool breeze on her skin.

"How is she doing?"

"She is a natural. She has been working very hard. I suspect that she wants to impress you. Her aim is excellent."

"And if she needed to rely on it?"

"It is difficult to say. It is one thing to shoot a target, but quite another . . ."

He didn't finish.

"Yes," she said. "I know."

Mohammed noticed her empty glass. "Would you like another?"

"No, thanks," she said. "I better not. I'm going to get some sleep."

"Very good, Miss Beatrix."

"There are some things that we need to do tomorrow."

"Whatever you need."

"There's going to be a delivery in the morning. A few things we're going to need."

He knew what she meant. "I will make the arrangements. Would you like me to put them in the armoury?"

"Yes, please. And can you have the jeep ready? I want to take Isabella out into the desert."

"Yes, of course. Anything else?"

"Yes," she said, looking up into the square well that was formed by the riad's walls. "We are going to need to improve security. I want cameras up on the roof and in the alleyway outside. And motion sensors, too. Do you know anyone?"

"Yes, I do. A soldier I served with has started a home security business. I can ask him."

"That's good. Money isn't a problem. We need to make it much more difficult if anyone decides to pay us a visit. It's too easy at the moment. We can't afford that."

"How likely is it that they will come?"

She sighed, feeling the knot of tension in her gut. "They're coming, Mohammed. It's just a question of when."

Chapter Six

Beatrix slept fitfully, her dreams stalked by fear. She woke several times, and with the clock showing four-thirty, the pain in her bones was such that she knew it was pointless to try and get back to sleep again. She took the blister pack of morphine tablets from her pack and swallowed two. There were only three left. She was going to have to go back to the doctor and get more. She sat in the bath for half an hour until the first infusion of dawn had lightened the sky that was framed by the walls of the riad. Then she dressed in black trousers and a black, sleeveless T-shirt with a thick, cable-knit jumper that she would discard when the temperature started to climb.

She stopped in the armoury. Abdullah had been as good as his word and the equipment had already been delivered. There were three crates of oranges and lemons stacked against the wall in the courtyard, and Mohammed was in the process of uncovering the weapons that had been hidden beneath the bed of straw upon which the fruit rested.

"Good morning, Miss Beatrix."

"How is it?"

He spread his arms. "It all looks very good."

He cleared an armful of oranges away and took out the TAR-21 that she had ordered. It was a futuristic bullpup assault rifle that had been designed for the Israeli infantry. She took it from him and hefted it in both hands. The bolt carrier group was placed behind the pistol grip to shorten the length of the rifle without sacrificing barrel length. The size of the rifle was perfect for turning corners in urban warfare. It would be perfect for fighting in confined spaces, too.

Spaces like the riad.

They uncovered the rest of the order.

There was an MK249 with a dozen one-hundred-round, soft-pack ammo bags, together with three additional box mags and a Surefire suppressor.

A Mossberg 500 shotgun.

An M110 sniper rifle with bi-pod.

Three dozen flash-bang and fragmentation grenades.

A crate of Claymore anti-personnel mines.

"I'll check everything," Mohammed said.

"Thank you. Is the jeep ready?"

"It is in the usual place."

"There was an MP-5 in the order . . ."

"It is in the armoury. Would you like me to get it for you?"

"I'll get it."

She went into the room that had once been the riad's *hammam*, the traditional steam bath. They had installed a series of shelves and hooks and a large gun cabinet. The Heckler & Koch was on the workbench next to a box of ammunition. She took a Glock, shoved it into the waistband of her trousers and then took the submachine gun.

She left it on the table next to the pool and climbed the stairs to Isabella's room. The door was unlocked. She opened it quietly and went inside. Isabella was asleep, lying with her arms spread wide and the sheets wound around her legs.

Beatrix crept across the room.

"Isabella."

She woke at once.

"You're dead. Right now. I killed you."

"Mummy!" she protested.

"Is this what I taught you?"

"No, I . . ."

"You have to be alive to threats, sweetheart. All the time. It doesn't matter what time of the day it is. It doesn't matter if you are awake or if you are asleep. What are you supposed to do last thing at night?"

"Block the door."

"That's right. Block the door. So what happened?"

"You're home," she said. "I thought . . ."

"That you'd be safe? You're *not* safe. There are still three of them out there. Until we've eliminated all of them, they are still a threat. Do you understand?"

"Yes. I'm sorry."

Beatrix relented a little, regretting the harsh tone in her voice. "It's alright. I'm only angry because I love you. And because the people we are dealing with are very, very dangerous. You know that, don't you?"

"Yes."

"Good. Get dressed. I've got a surprise for you."

Mohammed had parked the jeep in the street into which the alleyways and passages eventually led. Beatrix had stowed the H&K, the cartridges and two watermelons in a nylon duffel bag. She unlocked the doors and slung it into the back.

"Where are we going?" Isabella asked as they pulled out into the quiet street.

"Somewhere we won't disturb anyone," Beatrix answered.

They headed south. It was a little after seven in the morning, and the city was still rousing from its slumber. The traffic was sparse, and they cleared the usual bottlenecks without delay, breaking out onto the wider roads that terminated in the city like the spokes of wheel. In an hour they were out into the desert.

Beatrix wondered, again, if she was doing the right thing. She had started to doubt herself, and the hesitancy was beginning to nag. She had spent much of the last year on Isabella's training, accelerating the syllabus when she realised that her illness was progressing faster than it could be controlled. Her aim had always been to ensure that her daughter could defend herself, but lately she had admitted to herself that she had another motivation.

A selfish motivation.

What if the cancer made her unable to do what needed to be done? What would she do then?

The sun was climbing into the sky, and the heat was cranking up with every minute that passed. The landscape was spartan and homogenous, dunes as far as the eye could see, with the asphalt ribbon of the road the only sign of human interference. Beatrix drove for another ten minutes until she was satisfied that the long view in both directions would give her plenty of notice should anyone approach. She slowed, turned off the road and followed a narrow track into the dunes.

No time for doubt now.

She stopped, killed the engine and took the bag from the back seat.

"Come on," she said.

They walked a little way from the jeep. She dropped the bag and opened it, taking out the watermelons.

"Wait here."

She walked on, dropping the first watermelon on the sand fifteen paces from where Isabella was standing and the second another five paces farther. She walked back to her daughter, collected the nylon duffle from the ground and took out the MP-5, three full magazines and another box of 9mm rounds.

"Here," she said, handing it to her daughter.

Isabella took it in careful hands.

Beatrix held up a magazine. "Show me how to load it."

The girl hadn't used an H&K before, but she was smart, and after fumbling the magazine in the receiver for a moment, she found the right position and snapped it home.

"This is an MP-5," she said. "They are very powerful submachine guns. You need to get used to firing them."

Isabella grinned with anticipation.

"What should I fire at first?"

"First of all, you need to set the gun to automatic. You know how to do that?"

The girl pointed to the selector on the side of the gun. "Here?"

"That's right. Click it around to F."

Beatrix watched as Isabella did as she was told.

"You know what some people say the F stands for?"

"Continuous fire?"

"Yes, that's one meaning. The other is fun. Ready?"

"Yes. What am I shooting at?"

"The first watermelon."

Isabella opened the retractable metal stock and took up a confident stance.

"It fires eight hundred rounds a minute. That's thirteen rounds a second. Think about that before you pull the trigger."

"I can do it."

"Go on, then. Show me."

She fired, the rounds going high and wide and throwing up little plumes of sand that jagged away in a rough diagonal.

"Bend your knees and lean forward. You can't pussyfoot with it. You've got to manhandle it. Line up the sights on the watermelon and then hold the trigger down. Two seconds."

Isabella straightened her shoulder, lowered her stance and pressed her cheek against the gun, sighting the target. She held down the trigger and sent twenty-six rounds up range. The watermelon exploded in a fountain of juice and wet flesh.

"There you go," Beatrix said.

She looked at her daughter and the confident way in which she handled the weapon. She was so young, just barely a teenager, and yet she was completely comfortable with an automatic machine gun. Beatrix had given her that confidence, and she should have been able to extract a measure of pride from it, but that was not an easy thing to do. The doubts kept nagging away at her. At Isabella's age, she should have been interested in innocent things: music or clothes or boys. She should not have been able to field-strip a pistol, arm and throw a fragmentation grenade, run ten kilometres in less than forty minutes or know the best pressure points to disable a man.

The more she thought about it, the more it seemed like a perversion of her youth.

And yet . . .

That she knew how to do those things spoke to the excellence of Beatrix's tutelage. It meant that Isabella would be able to defend herself, if that ever became necessary. It meant that her likelihood of safety was improved.

But it also meant that the last innocence of childhood had been torn away from her.

Worse, it meant that it was her mother, who should have nourished and protected that unworldliness for as long as she could, who was responsible.

Beatrix's exile, all those days and months alone with the memories of her bloody career, had imprinted on her the notion that she was an implacable killer with no room for emotion. She had thought that she was a machine.

She knew, now, that she was not.

Isabella had taught her that.

What had she given her in return?

It was impossible not to feel regret about the lengths to which she had been forced to go in order to protect her daughter. The cost had been high. She wondered, again, as she watched as Isabella leaned into her stance and raised the MP-5, if it had been too high.

Beatrix drove them back into town, and at the junction where she would normally have turned left, she impulsively turned right.

"Where are we going?"

"It's only ten. I thought we could make a morning of it."

"Doing what?"

"How about some shopping?"

"Shopping?" Isabella gaped at her as if she had suggested something outrageous.

"What's so funny about that?"

"We've never been shopping together."

"First time for everything. You don't want to?"

"I didn't say that."

It had suddenly seemed like the most natural thing to do. The training had gone well, and Isabella had grown more and more adept with the MP-5. Her aim had graduated from chaotic to undisciplined, and by the time they had exhausted the ammunition, it had improved to reasonable. She had taken to the gun with impressive ease and was soon hollering with satisfaction as she started to nail the targets, her face full of wild joy.

Beatrix found that the image of her daughter with the gun was not one she wanted to carry in her head.

She resolved to overwrite it with other memories.

There was a plaza on Mohammed V Avenue that was full of clothes shops, and Beatrix drove them there. They spent two hours walking between high-end establishments, buying whatever took their fancy. Money wasn't a problem; she still had plenty from the remission she and Milton had extorted from Control before he tried to double-cross them. The riad was paid for, and there would still be enough for Isabella when she was gone, too.

Beatrix smiled happily as Isabella pointed to dresses, jeans and shoes that she liked, and then she bought all of them for her. Isabella relaxed once she had satisfied herself that this was really happening. All the untimely maturity that had been forced onto her by her disjointed childhood fell away, and she became exactly what she was: an excited thirteen-year-old girl.

There was a spa in the plaza, and to her surprise, Isabella grabbed her hand and dragged her through the doors. She was not one for places like that, but Isabella insisted.

"You always look tired," she said. "You should do something nice for yourself."

It had been ten years since Beatrix had allowed herself the luxury of a treatment. Her initial reservation when she arrived in Hong Kong had been that she didn't deserve it, then that it was frivolous, and then, as she chased the dragon into oblivion, that everything else was superfluous to her next hit. She would have denied herself the extravagance now, too, but Isabella was adamant.

"Come on," she said, tugging her hand.

"I don't know."

"I've never done anything like this before," Isabella said.

Beatrix frowned. "Never?"

Her daughter looked at her bashfully. "No," she said, a shy smile on her face. "Of course not."

That gave Beatrix pause. No, she reminded herself. When would she have had the chance? Her childhood had been a litany of institutions and foster parents.

That was all the reason she needed.

"Come on, then."

She paid for twin massages in the clinic's luxurious *hammam*, and as she lay down on the heated table and felt the masseuse's strong hands begin to knead away the hard knots of tension in her shoulders, she was overtaken by fatigue and quickly fell into a deep sleep.

———

There was a photo booth next to the entrance to the arcade. Isabella took Beatrix's hand and tugged her over to it.

"What?" Beatrix said.

"I don't have any pictures of us together."

Beatrix had avoided photographs for as long as she could remember. She had to remind herself that this was safe.

"Can we?"

"Of course we can. That'd be nice."

They dumped their bags next to the booth and squeezed inside. Beatrix put thirty dirhams into the slot and then grimaced at the blank screen. She could see her awkward reflection gazing back at her.

"Smile, Mummy. It won't kill you."

Isabella reached across and took her mother's hand.

Beatrix exhaled and smiled.

They went outside and bought coffees. They took them back to the booth as they waited for the photos to develop. Beatrix looked at her daughter and wondered, yet again, whether she was doing the right thing.

Her focus, her aims, the training.

Was it right?

Was it moral?

Was there an alternative?

Isabella sipped the coffee, a young girl trying to look older than she was, and Beatrix settled on the fact that she was doing the best that she could, doing what she thought was best, in a situation where there was no perfect answer. If the goal was Isabella's safety, then the end justified the means.

The booth whirred and deposited the strip of photographs. Isabella took it from the slot and tore it in two. She handed half to her mother and kept the other half herself.

Beatrix looked at the pictures: she was smiling, but it was to her daughter that her eye was drawn. Isabella had her arm around Beatrix's waist and her head was angled slightly against her mother's shoulder, her smile big and natural, easy. There was love in her eyes.

Beatrix felt her determination, freshly reinforced, waver yet again.

She touched the photographs, folded the strip nearly down the middle and slipped it into her pocket.

She steeled herself.

These were hard choices.

There was no right and no wrong.

It had to be done.

Chapter Seven

She had two appointments that afternoon. The first was with Johnny, the tattoo artist she had used for the two roses that had adorned the skin of her left arm. He was waiting for her in the salon not too far from the Jemma el Fnaa square.

"You ready for the next one?" he asked as she climbed the steps down into the basement.

"I am."

She took off her shirt and flexed her arm so that she could see the work that he had already done.

The first rose was for Oliver Spenser.

The second was for Joshua Joyce.

They had both been in her house when, nearly ten years ago, her husband Lucas had been shot and Isabella had been stolen away from her. The eight black ink bars that she had tattooed down her ribcage on the left-hand side of her chest recorded the years that she had been separated from her daughter.

The roses were beautiful: blood-red petals and twisting stems that prickled with thorns. She had explained to Johnny what she'd wanted done, and he had come up with a design that matched her intentions perfectly.

She said she wanted a design that would accommodate six roses. There would be blooms on her shoulder, on her bicep, others on the inside and outside of her wrist. When she was done, there would be a whole sleeve of them.

Halfway there.

Lydia Chisholm would be the third.

Bryan Duffy would be the fourth.

Johnny swabbed her arm and inspected the two roses that were already there. "These have healed nicely," he said. "Look good, too. You pleased with them?"

"Very pleased," she said.

She sat down on the couch as he finished sterilising her skin. He sat on his chair and kicked away from her, rolling on its castors across the room to his laptop. He pressed play, and "The Ecstasy of Gold" by Ennio Morricone started to play out through the speakers.

"You like Westerns?" he asked her.

"I'm not much into films."

"*The Good, The Bad and the Ugly.* Fucking brilliant, man. Tell me you've seen it?"

"Never have."

"You gotta."

She closed her eyes as the music faded out to be replaced by the brutal riffs of Metallica's "Creeping Death."

Johnny Ink fired up his tattoo guns and went to work.

The second appointment was with her doctor. Abdeslam Lévy had his surgery in the exclusive Palmeraie district of the city. One of the benefits of paying his eye-wateringly high fees was the ability to see him on short notice. She sat in the waiting room and stared blankly at the abstract art on the wood-panelled walls. The morning with

Isabella had been wonderful, but now that she had dropped the girl back in the medina, the pain had crept back into her bones.

It was always there, when she stood and when she sat, a reminder that the days she had left to her could be measured.

Everyone was going to die, but ignorance meant that the inevitable could be processed as an abstract concept.

She didn't have that luxury.

Beatrix's previous career had made her more familiar than most with the certainty of death, and she had been sanguine about the possibility that it might end with a bullet or the point of a knife. She could fight those. She could pit her skills against those seeking her end, and so far she had found that she was the equal of them all.

But this assassin couldn't be fought.

It had crept into her body when she was too broken and beaten to fight it. Now that she had something to live for, and the money to treat it, it was too late. The cancer sat there, deep inside her cells, mutating. They could slow its progress, but they could not stop it.

Lévy had estimated that she had a year. The way she was feeling now, she wondered whether that was optimistic.

The receptionist smiled politely at her and said that the doctor was ready.

She went through into the consulting room. It was tastefully and expensively decorated, a reminder that the bill for even this visit would be for three hundred dollars.

"How have you been feeling, Beatrix?"

"Not great."

"The pain?"

"Bad. Worse."

"On a scale of one to ten?"

The usual question. "Seven." Her answer was usually four or five.

"We might need to look at the pain relief plan, then. How are you getting on with the morphine?"

"I'm nearly out. I need more."

Lévy frowned and looked at his screen for her records. "Really? I gave you enough for a month ten days ago. How many have you been taking?"

"Enough so that I can cope."

"Two or three a day?"

"Sometimes."

"I'd much rather you didn't. You can take too much, Beatrix."

"Does it matter?"

"There are side effects. Dizziness. Confusion. Mood changes. Low blood pressure."

She laughed bitterly. "That would only be relevant if I had a future to worry about."

He looked at her with disapproval. "We need to have a look at how we are managing the pain."

"The morphine works. Just give me some more."

"No, I don't think so, Beatrix. I'd rather we have a look and see if we can't find something more suitable."

"I don't have time to do that today."

He sighed. "Then we need to fix a time when you do have time."

"I've only got two more tablets. I need something now."

He frowned again. "I'll give you a script to get you through the next few days, but I want you to come back in so we can talk about this properly. I'm not comfortable with the amount you're taking, Beatrix. Not at all."

He printed out the prescription and passed it across the desk.

"I understand," she said. "Thank you. I'll make an appointment."

Two days?

If she felt like this, it would be difficult to even *travel* to Iraq, let alone do what she needed to do.

Two days.

Two days was nowhere near enough.

41

Chapter Eight

The pharmacy she had in mind was in an upscale neighbourhood on the outskirts of the city. She often filled her prescriptions there, and she could remember enough of the layout to know that she would be able to get inside without too much bother. The windows and doors were secured by discreet metal bars, but she had no intention of gaining access that way. There was a narrow alleyway that bisected the block, with the pharmacy on one side and a boutique hair salon on the other. She passed into it, was quickly swallowed by the darkness. The row of shops were only a single storey high, and when she got to the end of the alleyway, there was a dumpster that, when she vaulted atop it, allowed her to reach up to the lip of the flat roof. Wincing from the lightning bolts of pain that lit up her nerves, she scrambled her feet up the wall and hauled herself onto the roof.

She lay there for a moment, staring up at the yellowing rind of moon as she tried to capture her breath. This weakness was so out of character for her that sometimes she wondered if she had been transplanted into the body of another, weaker, woman. There had been a time when she would have been able to make the jump to the roof without the dumpster. But that prospect now? It was a bad joke.

She rolled over onto her belly and then pushed herself to her hands and knees. There was a skylight directly in front of her. It was protected by a cage, but the padlock was cheap and flimsy. She unslung the rucksack that she was wearing over her shoulder and removed the set of short-handled bolt cutters that she had taken from the armoury. She pressed the teeth around the lock and brought them together. The arm of the padlock snapped, and it fell away.

She pulled the cage aside, used the handle of the cutters to knock a hole in the glass and reached through to open the latch. The skylight pulled back on rusty hinges, and she dropped down into the dark room below.

The cabinet where the drugs were stored was also locked, but that security, too, was not fit for its purpose. Unobserved, and with no alarms to concern her, Beatrix was able to pick the lock at her leisure. It took less than a minute.

She pulled the door open and looked at the neatly ordered boxes of drugs inside.

Morphesic SR.

MXL.

Zomorph.

Sevredol.

Oramorph.

She opened the mouth of her rucksack and started to drop the boxes inside.

⌣⌣

By the time she had returned to the riad, the effect of the morphine had taken hold. It numbed the constant drill of the pain to a dull throb. It did not remove it completely, but instead held it in the shadows, where it remained, crouched and patient, gathering strength and preparing to return. She was in no doubt that this wasn't anything other than a temporary reprieve.

Mohammed and his wife, Fatima, were eating in the dining room. Mohammed got to his feet as he saw her crossing the courtyard.

"Is everything alright, Miss Beatrix?"

"It's fine. Sit down. Finish your dinner."

"I've finished," he said, waving her concern away. "When are you leaving?"

"Tonight."

He gestured up towards Isabella's bedroom. "We will look after her."

"I know you will."

"My friend came this afternoon. He thinks the riad can be made much more secure. He suggests cameras and motion sensors on the roof and several cameras outside. He thinks it will be difficult for anyone to get in without giving us fair warning. Would you like me to go ahead?"

"Please. I trust you, Mohammed. Do what you think is best."

"Very good, Miss Beatrix." He paused and looked at her with concern. "Can I ask how you are feeling?"

"I'm fine," she said, more abruptly than she intended. She spoke more gently. "You don't need to worry about me."

"Be careful," he said. "She only just got you back again."

⌣

Beatrix tried Isabella's door. The handle turned, but only so much. It was catching on something. The room had a window that looked out onto the open corridor that ran around the riad and the courtyard below, and it was covered only with a thin gauze curtain. Beatrix looked through it and saw that a chair had been propped up against the door, jamming the handle. That was good.

She was about to leave when she noticed that the gauze curtain was pulled aside at the other end of the window. She moved over to it and looked inside. Isabella was lying on her side, her face turned to the window. She looked peaceful and innocent, and Beatrix wondered again whether it had been selfish of her to remove her from the foster parents.

But then she remembered the blank and emotionless mask that always fell over her daughter's face whenever they had discussed her childhood. A peripatetic existence, moved from one unloving home to another, no structure, no purpose. She needed to be with her mother. And Beatrix would do everything that she could to make sure that she was safe.

She was about to turn away when she saw that Isabella had something clasped in her right hand. She stared hard into the gloom of the room until she had identified the strip of photographs that they had taken that morning.

And then she turned away.

If she didn't leave now, she never would.

Chapter Nine

Pope had arranged for her to be flown under diplomatic cover from Marrakech to Kuwait City. They did not know how deeply Manage Risk was embedded into the security apparatus of southern Iraq, and so they decided to avoid having her name on the passenger manifest of a flight into the country. Instead, she would be driven across the border to Basra.

It had been agreed that she would be equipped when she arrived in Iraq, and so the only contraband items that she was bringing, her throwing knives, had been stowed with the rest of her gear in the hold. She passed through security with a minimum of fuss and boarded the waiting jet. They kept their take-off slot, and Beatrix watched with melancholy regret as the lights of the city disappeared into the uniform bleakness of the desert that surrounded it.

It was an unusual feeling.

She presumed that she had felt the same way when she had flown out of London into exile, but she could barely remember those days. The cause was easy to identify: the time left to her was starkly finite, and every day that she spent away from her daughter hurt like a wound. She stared into the cloak of pure midnight darkness that arched overhead. Those absent days hurt, but they were necessary. She had to keep moving.

They knew that she was back now, and they would be desperately trying to find her.

They had used Isabella to protect themselves once before, and she was sure that they would try and repeat the trick.

She would not let that happen.

She had downloaded as much information on Manage Risk as she had been able to find, and as the plane levelled off and the cabin crew began the preparations for supper, she took out her iPad and started to read.

Manage Risk had been established by Jamie King, a former Navy SEAL who had attended the Naval Academy and graduated from Hillsdale College. King sought to offer private security services to the governments and other companies operating in dangerous parts of the world. Its first major assignment was to provide thirty men with top-secret clearances to protect the CIA headquarters and staff engaged in the hunt for Osama bin Laden in Pakistan. Other clients included communications, maritime, petrochemical and insurance companies. The company had grown quickly and was organised into ten separate divisions, each dedicated to a separate area of business. It was registered in Mauritius, with minimal oversight of its accounts or corporate governance. Unsubstantiated rumours suggested it had contracts worth in excess of one hundred million pounds a year. Its website advertised its ability to provide "personnel from the best militaries throughout the world," and its tasks ranged from "personal protection to large-scale stability operations requiring large numbers of people to assist in securing a region."

At some point after she left Group Fifteen, Lydia Chisholm had been invited to join the board of the company, and she had established its affairs in the United Kingdom and Western Europe.

Joshua Joyce and Bryan Duffy had been recruited, too, taking senior operational positions. It was estimated that the company employed five thousand soldiers, many of them with a background in Special Forces.

A small army.

"Good evening, madam." The steward was smiling down at her. "Would you like a drink?"

Beatrix looked at the trolley.

"Whiskey, please. Rocks."

"Certainly."

The steward opened one of the miniatures and poured it into a glass. Beatrix thanked her, and then, when she had moved down the aisle, she took out the blister pack of Zomorph and popped out two of the tablets. She swallowed them, washing them down with the whiskey, and then put the iPad away and settled down to try and sleep.

Chapter Ten

B ryan Duffy was a big man. He was in his early forties and bristled with muscle from the time he spent in the gym that he had installed in his house in the upscale part of Basra. He was an ex-soldier, like the other mercenaries who worked for Manage Risk, and like many of them, he wore a big hillbilly beard that reached down to his sternum. An array of tattoos was visible on his arms and neck. He wore a black T-shirt and olive-green cargo pants, and there was an expensive diving watch on his left wrist. He was an impressive man with a lot of presence.

He was standing in the yard of the al-Mina prison. The space was bounded by two temporary Portakabins and the wall of the main prison building. There was a small table sheltered by a golf umbrella, and there was a monitor and three empty bottles of beer on the table. He had a half-finished bottle in his hand, and he took a long draw on it before he ducked down to look at the monitor, shielding his eyes against the glare of the morning sun.

The picture showed a young Iraqi prisoner, late teens or early twenties, dressed in a prison jumpsuit. There was an ugly bruise on the side of his face, and his nostrils were blocked up with dried blood.

"Fuck this shit," he said to Brent McNulty.

"Tell me about it."

McNulty was Duffy's number two. An ex-Ranger, a tough and hard-working man who had been employed by Manage Risk ever since he had left the military.

"You reckon any of them know anything?"

"Hard to say," McNulty said. "Sure as shit we got to find out one way or another."

"Yeah," he said. "This is my fifth one today."

He shrugged expressively. "Do I look impressed?"

"How many?"

"Nine."

"You want this one, too? Make it an even ten?"

McNulty grinned. "You're alright, boss. I'll have a beer and watch out here. Make it a good one. Maybe I can learn a little."

"Ah, fuck it. Sooner I get this over with, the sooner I can go home."

He finished the beer and handed over the empty bottle. He took a ski mask from his pocket and pulled it over his head. He started to sweat immediately. That always put him in a bad mood.

He opened the door to the hut and went inside.

⌣

He remembered the first time he had sat in on an interrogation. He had a strong stomach, but he had almost vomited from what he had seen. The sordid room, the puddles of urine and blood on the floor, the prisoner who had been beaten so badly that he had been dragged back to his cell, his head lolling insensately between his shoulders, the flesh on the soles of his naked feet scoured into one big red welt by the length of hose that the Iraqis had used on him.

He had sat in on hundreds of interrogations since.

He had conducted hundreds.

He saw them for what they were, now: a vital tool. It was a game. The prisoner had a piece of information that he didn't want to divulge. Duffy wanted the information. It was a battle of wills to see who came out on top.

Make it something impersonal like that, and the unpleasantness is easier to ignore.

All part of the game.

And Duffy always came out on top.

The inside of the hut was like all the others. The first thing that hit you was the heat. There was no ventilation, and even though the windows were blocked by blackout blinds, the sun still beat against the metal ceiling and cooked the air inside. And then there was the smell: a toxic mixture of sweat, urine and excrement, seemingly intensified by the temperature. There were two gaunt policemen from the Basra department, waiting to the sides. They were both sweating. They had spent five minutes working over the prisoner, softening him up. It was hot work.

There was a video camera on a tripod, its lens aimed at the man kneeling on the floor, his hands secured behind his back with cable ties. He was blindfolded. There was a bucket on the floor, a hose and a dirty towel.

Duffy took a clipboard from the table next to the camera.

"Let me see." Duffy looked down at a piece of paper on the clipboard. "What's your name? It's Faik, right?"

"Yes."

"Mr Faik al-Kaysi?"

"Yes."

"How old are you?"

"Twenty-one."

"Alright, then." He knelt down and untied the blindfold. The man had bloodshot hazel eyes, and he blinked at the sudden light. "Hello, Faik. Let me tell you how this is going to go down. I want you to listen to me when I'm talking to you. I want you to look at me. I want you to think very carefully about my questions, and I want you to give me honest answers. You understand?"

The boy glared up at him.

"If you don't do any of those things, there are going to be consequences for you. If you give me attitude, I'm going to make you sorry. If you are insolent, I'm going to make you sorry. If you lie to me—*especially* if you lie to me—I'm going to make you sorry you were ever born. Are you getting all this?"

The boy looked away.

Duffy slapped him across the face.

"You need to keep looking at me, Faik."

He glared back at him. There was fear in his eyes. That was good.

"Let me explain to you why I am here. You are under the jurisdiction of my friends from the Basra police department over there, but we think you might have some information that is helpful to my employers. Seeing as the Basra police and my employers have an excellent working relationship, they've agreed to let me have a talk with you. So we're going to have a chat, and you're going to help me out. You do that, maybe I can make things go a little easier for you. Are we clear on all of this so far?"

Faik glared at him.

"Yes or no, Faik?"

No response. Hatred seeped out of him like poison.

Duffy struck him again.

"Yes or no?"

"Yes."

"Alright. Now, first of all, I understand you have a complaint?"

"Your men, your *mercenaries*, they shot my mother."

"At the protest. Yes, I heard about that. Awful. It's a pity."

The boy's anger flared. "A pity? Is that all you can say?"

"You should watch your temper, Faik."

"Are the men being prosecuted?"

Duffy laughed. "Who?"

"The men who did it."

"No, Faik. They are not. There was an attack on a facility that is guarded by my company. The men responded appropriately. That is that. The protesters shouldn't have been there. And they shouldn't have attacked the gates. What happened next is their fault, not ours."

"I want to make a complaint. I demand that they be arrested."

"You are in no position to make demands, Faik. Look around." He swept his arm left to right, encompassing the awful room. "Look where you are."

"I want to . . ."

Duffy interrupted him. "No, Faik, it's my turn now. It's what I want."

"They beat me with my hands tied. Why should I help you?"

"Because they'll beat you again if you don't. You need to focus on me, Faik. I'm your only friend here. I could give up right now, walk out that door and not come back, but if I do that, they're going to throw you into a cell, and then there won't be anything that I can do."

"No," he said. "I have nothing to say. I did nothing wrong."

Duffy walked around the boy, slowly, and then leaned in close. "You took part in an armed assault on an Iraqi civilian installation. My colleagues have evidence to suggest that the operation was organised by the Promised Day Brigade. That's a terrorist organisation, Faik. You know what will happen to you if you are found guilty of being a member of a terrorist organisation, don't you?"

"I am not . . ."

He shouted over him: "It's time for you to shut your mouth, open your ears and answer my fucking questions."

The boy shrank away from him.

"Why were you and your mother protesting, Faik?"

"Because it is not right what they do."

"They?"

"The people who run Energy City."

"And what do they do?"

"The jobs at the oilfields—those are Iraqi jobs. They have always been Iraqi jobs. Why do they bring in foreign workers when it is Iraqis who should be doing the work?"

"That is a matter of economics. It's nothing to do with you."

"We are hungry. We have no money. All we want to do is work."

"You are a terrorist, aren't you, Faik?"

"No," he said.

"Tell me about the Promised Day Brigade."

"I know nothing about them."

"You're lying, aren't you?"

"No."

"You're lying!"

"No," he said, "I am not."

He took the photograph that was clipped on top of the list of prisoners and showed it to him.

"That there is Mr Muqtada al-Sadr. We know he's been behind the attacks on foreign companies. What I want from you is where you met him and where I can find him."

He paused.

Faik said nothing.

"Feel free to chip in."

"I don't know him."

"You do. I know you do. If you tell me where to find him, I'll make sure you get a cell to yourself tonight. A shower and a hot meal, too. You just have to tell me where he is."

"I do not . . ."

Duffy shook his head. "This is a real shame. I've been doing this awhile and it's always better if everyone is on the level, cooperating with each other. I was hopeful you might want to get yourself out of this mess. I'm disappointed in you." He straightened out the ski mask. "Alright. Have it your way. Next question: Why were you carrying an AK-47?"

The boy looked up at him with stunned eyes. "I was not."

"That's not what your file says. It says you were arrested with an AK and two full magazines."

"That is a lie. They are fabricating it."

"Do you want to think about my questions again? Tell me about the Promised Day Brigade. Tell me about al-Sadr."

"I know nothing about them, I swear it."

He sighed expressively. "Fine," he said. "I tried my best. Have it your way."

He nodded at the two Iraqi policemen, and they quickly moved from the back of the room to where the boy was seated. The boy tried to stand, but they were at his side, each taking him by an elbow and a shoulder and pushing him back down onto the floor. Duffy took a towel from the floor and draped it over the boy's face. He reached over to the tap on the wall, twisted it on, and took the hose just as the tepid, dirty water was starting to dribble out. He held the hose over Faik's face and the towel quickly became heavy and sodden.

"Muqtada al-Sadr is responsible for the attacks on foreign oil workers in Basra. You know where he is."

"I don't!" the boy said, gasping for breath.

He lowered the hose so that the water fell directly onto Faik's nose and mouth. "Tell me where he is and this can all stop."

"I don't know him!"

"Why are you protecting him?"

Faik tried to speak, but he could not.

"Where can I find Muqtada al-Sadr, you piece of shit!"

The boy coughed and spluttered again, and Duffy ripped away the sodden towel. Faik gasped for air.

"Pick him up."

The policemen did as they were told.

The boy's face and hair were wet. He looked much younger than before.

He coughed helplessly. His eyes shone with fear.

Duffy gripped him by the chin and tilted his head up so that he was looking at him. "How old are you?" Duffy said. "Really?"

"Nineteen," he said quietly.

"Nineteen. Sounds about right, Faik. I reckon that's the first truthful thing you've said to me all day." He let go of the boy's chin, and his head slumped forward, resting against his chest. He turned to the policemen. "Take him back to his cell."

———

Duffy left the hut and stepped out into the baking heat outside. McNulty was still there. He was sitting on an upturned oil drum, watching the monitor as the policemen fixed cuffs around the boy's wrists.

"You been watching?"

"Nothing better to do. What do you think?"

"He doesn't know anything," Duffy said. "He's just a kid. What do you think?"

"That would be my guess."

"Poor little bugger. He's going to get thrown into a cell, and then God only knows what they'll do to him."

"Not our problem," McNulty said, standing up and sliding his Ray-Bans onto his weather-beaten face. "You want to get another beer?"

Duffy had been doing this long enough to be able to compartmentalise his work. The interrogation was necessary, even if it hadn't produced anything useful other than that the boy knew nothing. And now it was done.

"Sure," Duffy said. "Why not."

Chapter Eleven

The airbus stopped in Doha to refuel before travelling on to Kuwait City.

She spent her time reading the dossier on Mackenzie West that Michael Pope had provided. He fit the profile of the typical Manage Risk operative: he had been a Ranger with experience in Iraq during the occupation. His file showed that he had enjoyed an exemplary career and had been recruited by the company as soon as he demobilised. There had been work in Pakistan, Afghanistan and then Iraq. His annual fitness reports were near perfect.

It appeared that he had enjoyed something of a Damascene conversion soon after his arrival in Basra, with his line managers reporting that his conscience was proving to be an impediment in the efficient fulfilment of his duties. They had insisted that he undergo a psychological evaluation, and the spooks at GCHQ had been able to hack into Manage Risk's servers and download it. The report had suggested that an incident on the road out of Basra in which an insurgent's IED had killed a colleague had provided the impetus for his change in outlook. What he had witnessed outside the gates of Energy City had been the final shove that he needed.

Now, the report said, he was unstable and could not be trusted to toe the company line. He was, they said, a liability.

They arrived in the evening, the dying sun casting its last rays across the expensive new airport. Beatrix had operated in the Middle East dozens of times before, but it was still a shock to the system to leave the climate-controlled interior of the Airbus for the heat outside. The air bridge was air-conditioned, too, but the evening's heat bled through it and slapped against the disembarking passengers as if it were a physical presence. Beatrix slugged back a mouthful of cold water from the bottle she had taken from the steward and walked purposefully to border control. Now that she was here, she wanted to get started. There was a lot that needed to be done.

She flashed her diplomatic credentials and bypassed the sweaty line that had formed at the understaffed gate. The airport stretched away, gleaming steel and chrome and marble. She bought another bottle of water from a concession, swallowed another Zomorph and negotiated the slowly revolving doors into the baking warmth outside.

She carried her bag to the taxi rank and slid into the nearest cab. It was blissfully cool inside.

"Where to?"

"The Intercontinental," she said.

Beatrix was waiting at the hotel bar as she had been instructed. It was a hot, stifling evening, and she had ordered a beer to try and combat it. The place was as weird as the rest of the crazy city: armed guards at the door and an atmosphere that was wound tight with apprehension. The other drinkers were going about their business with single-minded determination, as if they could find reassurance in the bottom of their glasses. She was wearing a pair of jeans and a sleeveless top that emphasised her lithe and muscular figure.

A man had been drinking next to her for the last five minutes. He was alone and she had noticed him casting cautious looks in her direction. She had angled her shoulders away from him and was about to take an empty table when he cleared his throat awkwardly.

"I'm Simon."

She nodded impassively.

"Can I get you a drink?"

"No, thank you."

He pointed at her empty glass. "But you've finished. Let me get you another one."

She turned to face him. Her eyes, icy powder-blue, were blank and pitiless as she stared at him. She could see the confidence that he had managed to assemble melt like the ice cubes in his glass. "No," she said. "Thank you. I'm fine."

He swallowed down his embarrassment and shuffled around on his stool.

"Excuse me."

Beatrix turned in the other direction, an exasperated retort on the tip of her tongue.

The man standing at the bar was in his early thirties. He was muscular, with thick arms that bulged through a grey T-shirt that was a little too small for him. He had a pair of Aviators pushed back on his forehead, and his black hair was cropped short, a number one buzz cut. His jaw was square and his skin was tanned.

"Miss Rose?"

"Yes."

"I'm Damon Faulkner," he said. "Michael Pope sent me."

Faulkner bought them both drinks, and they moved to a quiet table in the corner of the bar where there was less chance that they would be overheard. Beatrix watched as he brought the fresh pints across the room to her. He was obviously ex-military: he walked with the confident gait that she had come to expect in spec-ops guys and his appearance was straight out of central casting. He deposited the beers on the table and sat down.

"Good to meet you," he said. "Pope has told me a lot about you."

"Really?"

"I think he's a fan."

"That's nice," she said. "He hasn't told me anything about you."

He smiled. "I was in the Regiment for five years, until two months ago. That's when I got the tap on the shoulder, and they asked me if I was interested in transferring to the Group."

"What are you? Number . . . ?"

"Number Twelve."

"Twelve." The most junior member of the team.

"That's right. I understand there've been a few vacancies recently."

Five, she thought. Five traitors whom she and Milton had eliminated on the Russian steppes.

"How much do you know?"

"I know that Captain Pope's predecessor and some of his agents were corrupt."

"And what do you know about this?"

"This?"

"This. Why you're here with me."

"He wants me to get you into Iraq. Once we get to Basra, he wants me to get you equipped and then get you down to Rumaila."

"Anything else?"

"We're going to bring a chap across the border afterwards."

"Anything else?"

"That's all he told me."

Beatrix hadn't asked for help, but if Faulkner was decent, then perhaps it would be useful to have him around.

"Alright. What's your plan?"

"I'm parked outside. We'll wait until it's dark and then we'll drive west. Once we get to Basra, I'll fix up an appointment with the Group quartermaster. Should be able to get you kitted up with most of the gear you want. Sound alright to you?"

Chapter Twelve

Faik was taken back into the main prison building and led through the warren of corridors until he reached a small cell with thirty other men inside. There was a bench along one wall and a bucket for them to relieve themselves. There were no windows and the only light came from a flickering striplight high above.

The guards opened the door, covering the men with rifles, and tossed Faik inside.

The other prisoners paid him no regard. It was stifling hot, and the bruises that the policemen had inflicted were sore to the touch.

He sat down in a narrow space against the wall, bounded by two other men. He realised, with abject clarity, that his situation was very bad indeed. He felt lonely and helpless.

"Are you alright, brother?"

Faik looked up. The man to his right was looking at him.

"Are you alright?"

He gave a single stoic nod.

"What is your name?"

"Faik."

"I am Ahmed. You have been with the mercenaries?"

"How do you know?"

He pointed and added with a polite smile, "Your hair is still wet."

"They think I am with Muqtada al-Sadr."

"Are you?"

"No," he said. "I was protesting at Energy City. My mother was killed."

"I am sorry."

Ahmed paused for a moment. Faik took the chance to compose himself.

"What are you here for?" he asked him.

"I am a lawyer. I found evidence of fraud in the government. Bribes from big foreign corporations to win the contracts they tendered for. I was found out, and well"—he spread his arms—"here I am."

"But you didn't do anything wrong."

Ahmed looked at him as if he were a child. "That depends who you ask." He arranged himself against the wall, wincing from a stiff back. "They asked you whether you were with Muqtada?"

"Yes."

"What did you say?"

"That I didn't know him. And I don't."

"They don't expect us to say we do. I doubt they think we are involved in the uprising at all."

"I'm not."

"I believe you."

"So why are they asking?"

"It is all for effect. One big show. They need to show the people that they are serious about security. They will demonstrate that they can deal with the insurgents. It doesn't matter if the people they punish are engineers, office clerks, mechanics"—he gestured to himself and then to Faik—"or lawyers and young men."

Faik set his jaw and said with a conviction he didn't feel, "They'll let me out. They have to. I haven't done anything wrong."

Ahmed laughed, a hacking noise that soon became a hoarse cough.

"What?"

"You think they'll do it? Just like that?"

"Why wouldn't they?"

"They have to make an example of you now. Every time there is a protest or a shooting or a bombing, it makes it more expensive to do business here. They need to show the foreigners that they are serious about making it a safe place for them to work."

"But I can't stay here. My mother was . . . There are things I need to attend to. And I have a little sister. She is alone."

"She will have to learn to grow up, Faik. You will be here for many years."

"No . . ." He started to stand, anger twisting his face, until Ahmed reached over, took his shoulder and pressed him down.

"Be quiet, brother. If the guards think you are going to cause trouble, you will be beaten."

"I can't stay here."

"There might be a way."

"How?"

"You want to get out of here, brother?"

Faik suddenly found his eyes were full of tears. He tried to say that he did, but the words would not come. He nodded instead, blinking the tears back and swallowing hard.

"Like I said: I am a lawyer. I am going to represent as many of the prisoners as I can. If you like, I can add your name to the docket."

"Why would you do that? You don't even know me."

"Someone has to stand up for our rights. Some of the people in the government, I wonder sometimes whether they would prefer things as they were with Saddam. I would not. But we need to fight them. This is a good place to start, if Allah wills."

"What do I need to do?"

"Nothing. I am going to speak to the governor tomorrow. There are nine of us. If you like, you can be number ten."

Chapter Thirteen

Faulkner had a Land Rover Freelander parked in the short-stay car park. The gardens outside were well watered and healthy, but the road was barren and choked with dust that had been cooked in the sun all day. They drove for forty-five minutes out of the city, heading west, through a featureless desert landscape that looked almost lunar under the silvery starlight. They followed the same road that Saddam's tanks had used twenty-five years ago, eventually reaching the border at Safran. It was a broad, open car park with several four-by-four vehicles, a couple of trucks and a collection of Portakabins. There was no official transaction to speak of, and after Faulkner had signed a document for a clipboard-wielding functionary, they were on their way again.

"How safe is the road?" she asked as they accelerated away.

"Better than it was, but still not safe. There's a Glock in the glove compartment if you need a weapon."

"Are you armed?"

"I've got a Sig."

The landscape became more interesting the farther they travelled to the north. Route Eight was bleak and arid, just as in Kuwait, but now there were stretches that were littered with the carcasses of rusting tanks and other military vehicles, the detritus of war, a reminder of the fearsome power that had been ranged against Saddam's men. They raced through occasional villages composed of low-slung huts with corrugated tin roofs, surly residents standing in their doorways and watching with suspicious eyes as they hurried past. They didn't see another vehicle until they were well inside the border, and then it was just the lights of a military convoy moving in the distance.

"They say that the Garden of Eden was around here," Faulkner said as he turned onto the main road heading into Basra. "Joke, right? Maybe once, but I don't know about now."

Beatrix looked out. In the hazy distance she could see gas, the by-product of bringing oil to the surface, being flared. Other places might store that gas and use it, but here, with oil so plentiful, they just let it burn. The road was badly pot-holed, the traffic disorganised and disorderly, the motorists using the verge whenever a queue developed. As they passed into the fringes of the city, shops on the side on the road offered everything from construction materials to car repair. Small herds of sheep hovered around feeding troughs and waited to be sold. Camels crossed the road, seemingly oblivious to the peril that they were in. There were carcasses of dead vehicles, pools of fetid, stagnant water and more litter than Beatrix had ever seen in one single place. There were piles and piles of rubble. Beatrix remembered that from previous visits. The Iraqis never cleared rubble. They moved it to the sidewalk and left it there.

As they drew closer to the city, the number of soldiers increased. There were roadblocks every few miles on the road, but as they approached Basra, these became much more frequent. Iraqi soldiers stood behind reinforced concrete baulks, backed up by armoured cars with fifty-calibre machine guns. Everyone had to stop and show their papers.

"Been to Basra before?" he asked her as they pulled away from the latest checkpoint.

"No. Never been this far south."

"It's a total shithole. We never really got control of it. One thing about it, and it's pretty crazy, but you'll be able to tell the time just by opening your window and sticking your head out. You'll know it's seven in the morning from the explosions as the Iraqi patrols get hit by the IEDs that the insurgents planted overnight. It's like a fucked-up alarm clock. After that, you get the suicide bombers. And in the afternoon you'll get the mortar teams who like to lob bombs into the city itself. End of the day, you'll hear the small arms fire from the Iraqis going out on ops and the extra-judicial killings."

"I've been in war zones before," she said. "This won't be any different."

"If you say so."

Basra wasn't quite as bad as Beatrix had expected. They passed one of Saddam's large palaces with the outsized domes and the ceremonial battlements. There were Ba'athist statues, large and declaratory, surprisingly spared during the upheaval of the invasion. The streets were arranged in neat and ordered lines, the traffic within them surging forward with little regard to rules. Beatrix remembered the Iraqi standard of driving from Saddam's time. The main imperative was to keep moving, and if that meant driving on the wrong side of the road, going the wrong way around roundabouts or, occasionally, on the pavement, then so be it. It was anarchic, and Faulkner became quiet as he concentrated on avoiding a collision.

He accelerated away. "I've booked us into the Basra International. About the best you can find around here."

The hotel was in the Al-Ashar district in the north of the city, near to the Arvand River. They parked the Freelander in the car park and went inside. It was an old Sheraton and in reasonable condition, twin Iraqi flags flying from the flagpoles outside. Beatrix waited in reception as Faulkner took care of the papers. They had rooms on the fourth floor. Faulkner suggested that they take an hour to settle in and then meet in the restaurant for dinner.

The room was basic: a fake marble bathroom with a bath that obviously leaked badly in several spots, a claret-red carpet decorated with a gaudy golden design, thick drapes, faux-mahogany furniture, cheap prints on the wall. She dropped her bag on the bed and went over to the window. The view was to the southwest, towards Rumaila. She could see flame-topped derricks were visible, the nodding donkeys of the pumpjacks and the ubiquitous smoggy haze in the air.

It was close. A short drive away.

Duffy was there somewhere. It was very likely that he was expecting her.

That was fine.

It didn't matter.

She was coming anyway.

Chapter Fourteen

Faik had spent the day twitching with nerves. There was a sick feeling in the pit of his stomach. Ahmed's meeting with the governor had been scheduled for the morning. The guards came for him after breakfast, opening the door and escorting him away to the administration block. He clasped Faik's hand before he left.

"Don't worry, Faik. I can be a persuasive advocate. I can make a nuisance of myself. There is a saying: the squeaky hinge gets the oil. If I squeak enough, they will have to listen to me."

It would have been an exaggeration to say that Faik was reassured, but he did feel a little more at ease knowing that something, at least, was being done. He had slept badly that night, and he was still dead tired. There was a little more space in the cell now that Ahmed was out of the way, so Faik stretched out as much as he could, rested his head on his folded arms and tried to relax. He thought of his mother and his little sister, and eventually it was her beautiful face that he remembered as he drifted off into an uneasy slumber.

Faik awoke in the afternoon feeling a little more refreshed. He pushed himself up so that he was sitting against the wall and looked around him at the cell. The striplight overhead had finally died, and now the gloom was lit only by a shaft of light from the corridor adjacent to it. The other prisoners were either asleep or staring dumbly at the walls and the bars of their cage. Faik scrubbed the heels of his palms against his eyes in an attempt to wake up.

He looked around.

There was no Ahmed.

Had he been successful?

Where was he?

A guard was sitting in a chair in the corridor, a shotgun resting across his lap. He was snoring lightly, his sleep untroubled by the muffled cries of pain that could occasionally be heard from the direction of the interrogation block.

A group of six men sat together, and Faik eavesdropped on their conversation. They were talking about Ahmed, and he gathered that they were among the prisoners that he was representing. They noticed that he was listening, and once he had explained that he was one of their number, they invited him to join them. He picked his way over the out-flung limbs of prisoners who passed the interminable time in sleep and sat down amid them.

They introduced themselves: an oil worker, an accountant, a shopkeeper, two engineers and a driver.

"What do you do?" the accountant asked him.

"I am trying to find work."

"What does your father do?"

"He was a soldier."

"And you don't like the idea of that?"

"No," he said.

The men laughed.

"No indeed. A most dangerous profession."

71

"I was at the oilfield. I want to work there."

They scoffed.

"Good luck. Those jobs are not intended for Iraqis."

The accountant indicated the busy cell. "We were wondering where our advocate has gone."

"Maybe he has negotiated his own release and forgotten about the rest of us."

Faik's eyes went wide. "Do you think he . . . ?"

"Relax. It was a joke."

"He is an honourable man."

"Do you think he will be able to get us out?"

"I don't know. But anything is worth a try."

The guard outside the cell was listening to their conversation. He opened his eyes, stretched and yawned. "I wouldn't set too much hope in your friend Ahmed," he said. "He won't be able to help you."

"Why not?" asked the engineer.

"Because he's not coming back, friend."

"What do you mean?"

"The governor doesn't take kindly to being lectured by *criminals*." He spat the last word with eloquent distaste. "He sent the good lawyer to the interrogation block before lunch. I heard he had a heart attack and, well . . ." He allowed his tongue to poke out of his mouth and angled his head to the side.

"They killed him?"

"His heart, like I said. Tragic."

Faik struggled to his feet and ploughed through the others to the cell door.

"Let me out," he yelled at the guard. "I've done nothing wrong. I shouldn't be here."

He wrapped his fingers around the bars and started to rattle the door.

The guard rose from his chair. "Get back, boy," he said.

"I'm not a criminal. They shot my mother!"

He shook the door again, the metal clanking loudly.

The guard reversed his shotgun and drove the butt, hard, against Faik's fingers. His right hand flashed with sudden pain, and he let go of the bars.

The guard spun the shotgun again and pointed it at him. "Sit down, boy," he said with naked menace. "You don't want the same thing to happen to you, do you?"

Chapter Fifteen

The restaurant was rudimentary. They took a table near the window with a view across a parched lawn to the concrete blocks that had been deployed to stop car bombers from getting too close to the main building. The hotel was inhabited by plenty of Westerners, and it would have been a fine prize for the insurgents. Private guards, armed with automatic rifles, were stationed outside. Beatrix watched them for a moment and was not impressed. It would have been a simple thing to get past them.

To the left was the river, where motorboats and fishing skiffs churned through the sluggish brown silt. There was a freighter that had turned turtle off the main dock and bullet-marked buildings on the foreshore were reminders that this was until recently a city at war.

They waited for the waiter to bring them their menus.

"What's your story?" Beatrix asked him.

"What? Before the Group?"

"Sure."

"Special Boat Service."

"And before that?"

"Just a grunt. Did my time, here and there. Nothing special."

"You must have something. You made Special Forces."

"Must have gotten lucky."

False modesty. She ignored it. "What have you done so far for Pope?"

"Nothing. I've been training for six months. This is the first thing."

Beatrix had realised that he was green, but there was green and then there was *green*. She wasn't interested in babysitting a rookie. Faulkner must have read her concern.

"I know what I'm doing," he said, a little indignantly.

"I'm sure you do," she said, although she knew from experience that a career in Special Forces and a career in Group Fifteen were very different things. The former did not adequately prepare for the latter. It provided minimum baselines for physical and tactical capabilities, but active service in the Group required a certain mental state, an ethical flexibility, that came only with experience. It was something that was absorbed, the way that radiation seeped into the bones, slowly mutating the cells until the agent became something else entirely. It was a contamination. Faulkner, young and used only to stark blacks and whites, would not yet have been exposed to enough of it. She would have to remember that.

He was looking at her curiously. "What happened in Russia?"

"How much do you know?"

"I know half the Group were killed."

She nodded.

"And that you were involved."

She looked at him, as he was looking at her, and she nodded again. "Group Fifteen had a serious problem with vermin. An infestation. The man who was Control before Pope was the worst of all. He tried to kill me. He killed my husband and kidnapped my child. He tried to kill the agent who was Number One after me, too."

"John Milton?"

"That's right. You've heard of him?"

He gaped. "Of course I have. He's a legend."

Beatrix smiled. Green *and* starry-eyed.

"How many did he send?"

"He sent six to take us out. We sent six back in body bags. I expect Pope is working hard to replace them."

"He didn't say very much. I knew something had happened, but it's not like what I'm used to. There's no banter. I haven't even met any of the other agents."

"And you won't, or at least not very often. You work alone most of the time."

The waiter appeared with their menus. There was an ex-pat in the kitchen, but he was hamstrung by the selection of ingredients that were available to him. They ordered steak and chips, and when the food came, Beatrix found she was very hungry.

She set about her steak. "I need equipment," she said between mouthfuls.

"The Group has a quartermaster operating out of Basra. He'll get you whatever you need. We'll go first thing tomorrow."

"And then?"

"I thought we could take a drive out to Rumaila. Take a look around."

They ate in silence for a moment.

"Do you want to tell me what your plan is?" he asked her.

"What do you want to know?"

"I don't even know exactly what you're here to do."

"Two things."

"I know what I'm here to do: get Mackenzie West out of Iraq."

"That's the first thing. What do you know?"

"Just what Pope told me: that he wants to go public about the way Manage Risk are behaving with the locals. And that we want him to do that so he can cause them a headache."

"That's right."

"But that's Pope's agenda, isn't it? The government's? What are you here for? The second thing?"

"The vermin problem."

"There's a rat here?"

She nodded. "A particularly nasty one. A man who works for Manage Risk. Bryan Duffy. He and I have unfinished business. I need to be alone with him for five minutes."

"The kind of meeting where two people go in and one person comes out?"

"You've got the idea."

"Alright, then. That's all I need to know."

"You've got no problem with that?"

"I wouldn't be in the Group if I did, would I?"

"No," Beatrix said. "You wouldn't."

Let's see, she thought. *Let's see if you still feel that way when it's time.*

"Which order do you want to go after them?"

"I don't think it makes much difference. Duffy knows I'm coming."

"So what's first?"

"Let's have a look around tomorrow. I might get an idea."

———

They had a drink after their meal, and then Beatrix excused herself and said that she needed to rest. Faulkner stayed at the table, finishing his beer. He paid the check, stood and, making sure that she had gone up to her room and wasn't waiting in reception, went outside to the parking lot. He got into his Freelander and drove the short distance into downtown Basra.

He parked on the Corniche al-Basra, near the Lion of Babylon square. The area was busy with people, and traffic rolled alongside, impatient horns sounding. The buildings nearby were pocked with bullet holes, and there were deep, untidy piles of rubble all about. The street lamps overhead flickered on and off, casting intermittent puddles of light down onto the sidewalk.

The passenger door opened and Captain Michael Pope slid into the seat. He was wearing a white *dishdasha*, a long Iraqi robe that reached down to his ankles. A scarf was pulled up over his mouth and nose. He pulled the scarf down.

"Good evening, sir," Faulkner said.

"How did it go?"

"Fine. I picked her up and brought her across."

"How is she?"

"Combative."

"I know that, Twelve," Pope said impatiently. "Physically?"

Faulkner was puzzled. "She looks alright. Why?"

"You don't think she looks ill?"

"She's thin," he said, "but ill? I don't know. Can't say I noticed."

"Keep it in mind," Pope said. "You're going to spend time with her. More than I have. Something's not right and I can't put my finger on it. And if I'm right, I need to know about it. Alright?"

"Yes, sir."

He shifted, the robe tightening so that Faulkner could see the shape of a holstered weapon beneath his armpit. "What's your plan for tomorrow?"

"I'm going to get her equipped, and then we're going to go and have a look at the oil field. If I can persuade her to go after your man first, I will."

Pope nodded his approval. "Keep her focussed on that. Promising that she would get him out was the *only* way I could have this cleared. I cannot afford for this to go wrong."

"I understand, sir."

Pope pulled the scarf up around his mouth again.

"Keep me on top of everything and if you need me, call. But no one else can know I'm here. As far as SIS is concerned, I'm in London."

"Yes, sir."

He opened the door and disappeared into the busy night.

Chapter Sixteen

Beatrix managed a broken night's sleep and finally gave up the pretence at six. She rose, showered in the lukewarm dribble that was the best the hotel could manage and dressed in a white sleeveless T-shirt, black pants and black boots. She collected her Oakleys from the dresser and went down to the restaurant, where she had fruit and toast for breakfast, washing down two Zomorphs with a glass of tepid orange juice.

Faulkner joined her as she was flipping through an out-of-date copy of the *Herald-Tribune*.

"Ready?"

She nodded.

He drove her to downtown Basra. They stopped at a money changer and swapped some of her dollars for Iraqi dinars. They continued to a tailor's workshop, and he told her that she was expected. Faulkner drove off to take care of the paperwork for their drive to the oilfield, and she went inside. A man was working with a large bolt of fabric, measuring it out and then using a pair of long-bladed scissors to shear off the amount that he needed.

She cleared her throat.

He looked up. "Miss Rose?"

"Yes."

"Number Twelve said you were coming."

"What's your name?"

"That doesn't matter, does it?"

"No," she said. "Just that the quality of your merchandise is as good as it needs to be."

"Then you need not worry. It is."

Beatrix knew that the Group had quartermasters positioned around the world. They assimilated themselves into local society and surfaced only when called upon to kit out agents when they were in the field. She had met plenty of them during her career, but it had been years since she was active, and so it was no surprise that this man was new to her. He led her into a smaller room at the back of the workshop. There were finished suits hung on hooks on the wall and a large canvas bag on a table.

He unzipped it and took out an FN F2000 Tactical TR compact assault rifle. Beatrix picked it up and hefted it. It was a gas-operated, fully automatic and ambidextrous bullpup rifle, equipped with both an optical sight and an under-slung lightweight 40mm grenade launcher. She field-stripped the weapon down to its component parts and inspected each of them carefully. She reassembled it again.

"You won't get much smaller or more mobile than that," the quartermaster said.

"Ammunition?"

He took ten 30-round magazines and five grenades from the bag and put them on the table. "It is good?"

"Very good. Secondary weapon?"

"There you have a choice."

He laid out a Glock 17 and a Sig Sauer P226 Tactical. Both were 9mm pistols, and both had been fitted with custom suppressors. The quartermaster took out magazines for each weapon and laid them out. Beatrix took the Sig and broke it down, quickly pleased with it. It was almost box fresh. The Glock looked as if it had seen more action, and when she broke it down, she confirmed it. The parts were worn and in need of attention. The Sig was the better bet.

"And the rest?"

He retrieved a set of head-mounted LUCIE night vision goggles, six M84 flash-bang grenades and two canteen pouches for carrying them, a length of Cordex detcord, a No. 6 plain detonator, a small amount of C4, a roll of double-sided tape, binoculars, a handheld GPS unit with spare batteries and a combat first aid kit.

"Is that everything you need?"

"This is good," she said. "There's one other thing."

"Yes, please, what is it?"

"I need a small GPS tracker and a receiver."

"I have a commercial model. Quite reliable." He went over to a cupboard and took out a small black box that was about the same size as a cigarette lighter. It had a peel-away adhesive strip on one side. "It works with a smartphone."

"Do you have one?"

"Of course." He took a white box from a shelf, opened it and took out an older model iPhone. "This is unregistered. The tracker app is already installed."

"That's fine." She replaced the phone in the box and added it to the other items. "Thank you."

Beatrix hoisted the bag of equipment over her shoulder and went outside onto the street. This part of the city was heaving with new money. Oil money. The road was wide, almost a boulevard, and had been cleared of the rubbish and rubble that scarred so many others. Instead of bomb craters and decades of putrid refuse were new cars and touts hawking trinkets. There were garish new shop fronts selling everything from Turkish shawls and Gulf fragrances to Lebanese sweets. Photograph shops displayed photos of chubby babies. Cigarettes, carbonated drinks, fruit, bolts of cloth and cans of petrol were piled in tottering heaps across the pavements. Neon lights were everywhere, and the streets were thronged with shoppers. Restaurants had posters offering strangely coloured kebabs.

There was a shop selling colourful veils and gowns next to the tailor's. She stopped inside and bought an *abaya*, a dark cloak which was worn over the clothing and obscured its wearer from the top of the head to the ground. The synthetic fibre was lightened with colourful embroidery and handfuls of sequins. Beatrix was not interested in its decorative effect. It offered anonymity, and that was a gift that she suspected might be useful before she was through.

She saw the Freelander. Faulkner pulled out of the frenetic traffic and parked alongside.

"Get what you needed?"

She nodded, dumped the bag in the back and climbed up into the front.

"Want to have a look around town?"

She nodded, then sat back and looked out of the windows as Faulkner drove them out of the city. Basra's buildings reminded her of the old Soviet style of architecture, with boxy and uninspiring construction arranged in careful order. The Russians had pumped money into the country in the seventies, and this was their lasting legacy. The buildings could have been in Finland or Warsaw, save that the plain concrete walls were stained a dirty yellow by years of exposure to the sand and the dust. A few apartment blocks were enlivened by touches designed to elicit local custom, some of them even sporting Assyrian-style bas-relief etched onto the walls. But most were utilitarian and functional, with rusting air-conditioning units breaking up the straight lines.

The streets were busy with life. Taxis nudged and edged into the never-ending flow of traffic, their orange bonnets and boots dinged and dented from numerous collisions. Youngsters hauled wonky carts that were piled high with sacks of grain. A donkey staggered beneath the weight of the baskets of coke that had been balanced across his back. They saw a flock of sheep grazing on the sun-blasted grass of a roundabout, oblivious to the clatter of traffic that circulated around them.

"Let's go out to the oilfield," she said.

Authorisation was needed to get out to the oilfields to the south-west of the city. There had been numerous attacks on the facility by insurgents, and now that Manage Risk were engaged in providing security, it was vice tight. Faulkner had arranged the fake clearance; the papers were made out in Beatrix's name. The documents had been slid into in a plastic sleeve and placed on the dash.

They were halfway to the oilfield's administrative buildings in Energy City when they passed a large armoured vehicle parked at the side of the road. They were twenty feet beyond it when Beatrix heard the throaty roar of its big three-hundred-horsepower diesel engine turning over. She watched in the mirror as it rolled onto the road and started after them. There was a sign on the front, in both English and Arabic, that threatened "lethal force" if traffic got too close or didn't move out of the way. It sounded its horn, and the soldier in the roof turret waved for them to pull over.

"Here we go," Faulkner said anxiously, looking in the mirror.

It was a Grizzly armoured personnel carrier, a big infantry carrier designed for urban combat. The steel armour was painted jet black and angled into a V-shape to deflect explosive blast waves. There were multiple gun ports and a ring-mount roof turret with a soldier standing behind a 12.7mm machine gun. It was a beast of a vehicle, fast and almost impregnable. The Manage Risk logo, a Roman legionnaire's helmet before two crossed gladii, had been affixed to the flanks.

"What do they want?"

"Take it easy," Beatrix said.

"We've got gear in this car we won't be able to explain."

"I know we do. Pull over."

Faulkner slowed and parked at the side of the road. They were adjacent to an enormous nodding donkey that squeaked loudly every time the big head dipped down and back up again.

The hatch in the Grizzly's flank opened, and two private soldiers stepped out. They were dressed all in black, and both wore wraparound shades that obscured their eyes. They were equipped with M4 carbines, and they toted them as they approached, one on either side of the jeep.

"If they search . . ." he began quietly.

"They won't," she interrupted. "Leave it to me."

The soldier on Faulkner's side of the jeep spoke first. "Where are you going?"

"You can talk to me," Beatrix said.

"That right? And who are you?"

"Juliet Watson," she said, using the false name that they had used for the permit. She spoke with authority.

"Take your glasses off, please, miss."

"I will if you will."

The man frowned, but did as she asked. She removed hers in return.

"That's better," she said.

"So? Where are you going?" He was American, a low drawl of an accent that she guessed was from the East Coast.

"Down to the oilfield."

"No, you're not."

"We have a permit."

"What for?"

"I work for the BBC. The news division. You've heard of the BBC, haven't you?"

"Of course."

"We're filming a piece about the oilfield."

"What about it?"

She smiled at him as if he was simple. "You know this is the biggest reserve in the world, right?"

"Yes."

"So we're doing a piece about that. About the effect it'll have on the local economy. About the opportunities for the Iraqis and the companies contracted to get the oil out of the ground."

"It's been cleared with the authorities."

"I don't know anything about that."

"Would you expect to have been told?"

He shrugged.

"Want to see the paperwork?"

She took the plastic folder and handed it to him. The man opened it and shuffled dubiously through the sheaf of papers inside. They were fake, but they were good fakes. How was he possibly going to be able to tell? He glanced at the papers, but she could see that he wasn't really reading them. He was trying to work out what he should do next.

"Do you need to speak to your commanding officer?"

"No," he said, defensively. "This is my road. I got authorisation. Don't need to speak to no one else."

"That's great. Can we go, then? I've got to start filming this tonight, and I need to scout a location. I could really do without the hold-up."

He looked across the cab of the jeep to his mate, who was still wearing his dark glasses. The man shrugged back at him.

"Ah, shit, why not. But stay on the road, alright? There are plenty of minefields on either side. You go the wrong way, you're liable to get blown to kingdom come."

"Got it. Thanks."

Faulkner put the jeep into gear again, and they left the two soldiers standing on the side of the road.

"They're well equipped," she assessed, "at least when it comes to gear. Maybe not the smartest soldiers on the planet."

"They get better," Faulkner assured her.

Chapter Seventeen

The closer they got to the oilfield, the more Beatrix could smell the money. It oozed from deep under the featureless expanse of desert where oil derricks and natural gas wells sprouted among sand and scrub. Flames gushed high above them, and the air was thick with smoke and the acrid stench of burning.

They passed through makeshift villages of narrow metal-sided buildings that rose from the dunes, temporary housing to accommodate the workers who were needed to exploit the largest claim of crude oil in recent history. Shiftless children were gathered on the street corners, staring at them as they drove by. Beatrix would have expected the townships to be prosperous places, but they were not. They looked dirt poor.

Faulkner slowed as they approached a huge compound surrounded by two-metre-high walls. A sign next to the gates declared that it was Iraq Energy City and that trespassers would be shot. There was a tall observation tower on stilts, and a soldier with a sniper rifle watched from the accommodation at the top.

Below him, a large crowd had gathered by the gate. It was composed of men and women, all of them yelling abuse at the thirty or so Manage Risk guards facing them on the other side of the gate.

The guards were armed with sidearms and batons that they wore through loops on their belts.

"What is this?" Beatrix asked.

"The facility? They just finished building it. It's offices for the companies with a stake in the field. Accommodation for the foreign workers, too."

The protesters were chanting loudly. There must have been four or five hundred of them, and the mood was fraught and tense.

"You know what that's about?"

"There's been a lot of protests like this. The locals say they're not getting a fair shake when it comes to the new jobs. They're probably right. They're bringing senior management over from the west, and the workers are transferring from fields in Libya, Saudi, Qatar. They prefer people they know. They don't trust the locals. But these fields used to be owned by the people around here. They say they're being driven out."

She took out the field glasses and put them to her eyes.

Her heart jolted. "Shit."

She pressed the binoculars tight to her eyes and looked again.

"What is it?"

"Stop the engine."

He did as she asked, and she opened the door and hopped down.

"What is it?"

She ignored him and went around to the back. She opened the bag and, as discreetly as she could, took out the Sig, pressed in a fresh magazine and then pushed it into the waistband of her trousers. She took the *abaya* and pulled it over her head.

"Rose," Faulkner said. "Stop. What is it?"

She balled her fists, clenching and unclenching impatiently. "It's Duffy," she said. "Over there. Behind the gate."

Faulkner turned to look. There was no reason why he would recognise Bryan Duffy, but similarly, there was no way she could ever forget him. He was standing behind a line of soldiers, directing them. He was obviously the most senior man present. He was in command. She stared at him, remembering the way his hair swept back from his temple, the sharp nose, even the way he moved. He had grown a wild beard since the last time she had seen him, but it couldn't disguise his identity.

Faulkner suddenly looked very nervous. "Are you sure?"

"Completely."

"What are you going to do?"

"Just get a little closer."

"Don't forget about . . ."

"Don't forget about Mackenzie West," she finished for him, "Don't worry. I won't."

She walked to the back of the crowd. Her Arabic was excellent, and she understood the chants. They were loud and angry, declaiming the Americans for their imperialism and demanding jobs for local workers. The men and women thrust out their fists and stabbed upwards with the placards that bore their slogans. A cheer sounded to Beatrix's left, and she saw a flash of flame as a barrel-chested man set fire to the Stars and Stripes, inky smoke curling into the scorched air. The cheer was taken up by the others until it became a bellow of rage.

She stared through the forest of limbs and the bars of the gate at Duffy, and the flame of her hatred flickered and caught hold.

Another group of workers joined behind her. The atmosphere was febrile and capricious, and seemingly at the flick of a switch, it curdled from rowdy to ugly. The newcomers surged at the gate, and Beatrix was pressed deeper into the throng. She was heaved right into the middle, the eddies and currents of the crowd drawing her ahead against her will. She found the man with the burning flag to her right and a girl, incongruously young, small and fresh faced, to her left.

She turned her head. She couldn't see Faulkner anywhere.

The crowd pressed up against the gates, hands laced around the bars, and started to yank at them.

The chanting became angrier.

Beatrix tried to force her way back again, but the men and women behind her were pressed too tight, and there was nowhere for her to go.

She was less than twenty feet away from Duffy now. She was the only Westerner in the crowd.

A man in front of her tripped and fell, and she was pushed into him, stumbling, and reached out for support against the shoulder of the protester to her left. The fallen man reached up himself, his fist closing around the *abaya* and, tearing at it, yanked it down so that it fell away from her face.

She tried to rearrange it, but the crowd was constricting, and her arms were pressed against her sides.

If Duffy turned in her direction, if he saw her . . .

There was a screech of metal as one of the gates was pulled away from a hinge. The crowd yelled in jubilation, and the men at the front redoubled their efforts. The second hinge popped out, and the gate was thrown into the yard, forcing the guards to retreat.

Beatrix looked over at Duffy. He fell back, yelling something that she couldn't hear. The guards drew the batons from their belts and surged forward, meeting the crowd on top of the wrecked gate. The tenor of the protests became angrier as the shouting was punctuated by the deadened *thwack* of the batons crashing against skull and bone.

The man with the burning Stars and Stripes threw his smouldering pole like a javelin and rushed at the guards, bellowing in fury. Beatrix was jostled again, bumping into the little girl and knocking her over. She saw her face, looking up in terror as the stampede swarmed around her, and she realised that if she didn't do something, the child would be trampled underfoot.

She was pushed into the crowd again, but she pivoted, narrowing her profile, and shot out a hand. Her fingers fastened around the girl's wrist, and she wrenched her up into her arms and edged into a gap in the scrum, forcing a passage out to the side of the crowd. The first few yards were treacherous, and a guard's baton pummelled her arm as she shielded the girl's head. A second blow clattered against her forehead, dizzying her. The guard drew his arm back again, but Beatrix was faster, straightening her fingers and supporting them underneath with her thumb, driving her hand like a dagger into his larynx. He dropped to his knees, unable to breathe, his hands fluttering at his throat.

She kept moving, clutching the girl to her breast.

Once she was out of the mêlée, it was easier to move. She broke free of the crowd below the gatepost. A fully fledged battle was underway inside the gates until, as Beatrix picked the girl up and carried her out of the way, a single rifle shot rang out from the observation tower. The brawling paused, and then there were screams of terror as the protesters staggered back away from the gate, leaving a wide circle around the body of the man who had burned the flag in its centre. Beatrix saw a flash of red on his scalp but did not wait.

A second shot echoed back.

Two Grizzly APCs had pulled up at the gates, and men with automatic rifles were disembarking.

She needed to get away from here right now.

She looked for the jeep.

It was gone.

Faulkner must have been moved on by the security detail.

The short battle was over now, and the Manage Risk men were beginning to round up the protesters.

A meat wagon drew up.

More armed men disembarked.

Beatrix couldn't afford to be arrested.

The girl slipped her small hand into hers and pulled her away from the gates.

"We must get away from here," she said, as if reading Beatrix's mind.

"Where?"

"Come with me."

Chapter Eighteen

Beatrix followed the girl. She walked quickly, with a determined stride, and led her a quarter mile away from the facility, heading south. She didn't speak. Beatrix fixed the ripped *abaya* as best she could, managing to obscure the fact that she wasn't local. A couple of extra Grizzlies rumbled past, but the girl reached up and took Beatrix's hand again, and they paid them no heed. Beatrix's face was obscured by the shawl, and they would have looked like a mother and her child.

"Who are you?" the girl asked her as they walked.

"My name is Beatrix."

"You are not Iraqi."

"No."

"American?"

"English."

"You speak excellent Arabic."

"Thank you. I've had a lot of practice. What's your name?"

She looked across at her doubtfully, as if her name was something to be guarded. "It is Mysha," she said at last.

"Hello, Mysha. Thank you."

"For what?"

"For helping me. That was getting very unpleasant."

"No. I must thank you. I was going to be trampled."

"You shouldn't have been there. How old are you?"

"Twelve."

"Then you definitely shouldn't have been there."

She ignored that. "What about you?"

"What about me?"

"Why were you there?"

"I'm a journalist."

"The television?"

"Yes."

"You were there to report on it?"

"That's right."

She was quiet, as if musing on Beatrix's answer.

Another Grizzly went by, and then a series of police cars, lights flashing and sirens howling. Beatrix knew she had to get off the street. If Duffy had seen her, and that was more than possible, then he would put men into the area to look for her. Her disguise was rudimentary, at best. It wouldn't hold up. She had to get into cover.

They walked on and reached one of the small shantytowns that Beatrix and Faulkner had driven through earlier. It was comprised of sun-baked mud huts and lean-tos that looked like they would collapse with the faintest breath of wind. Some had corrugated metal roofs; others were wrapped over with mismatched tarpaulins. The houses were penned in by piles of scrap metal and bright green lakes of raw sewage. The streets were thick with rubbish, sickly sweet as it rotted in the heat. There would occasionally be a break in the line of huts, and the gap would be stacked high with trash, black plastic bags that had been ripped open by hungry animals, spilling their fetid contents into a thick, cloying soup. A mangy dog slunk across the road, his belly on the dirt. Two rats followed him. They passed a girl drinking from a broken water pipe. There was a woman perched on the piles of trash, picking out and emptying plastic bags. The other women wore *hijabs*, many in colours other than the usual black, perhaps in an attempt to inject a little vibrancy into what must have been a monotonous, difficult existence.

"Where are we?"

"We call it Kassra," the girl said.

Beatrix translated. "Broken?"

"Yes. The village next to it is Attashis."

"Thirsty. Broken and Thirsty."

"Yes."

The child led her through a maze of jumbled streets to a medium-sized hut with an orange tarp hauled over the frame to serve as a roof. The place was in poor condition. The ditch that ran at the back of the property was littered with packing crates and plastic bottles. Sewage ran along a trench in the middle of the road. The walls were constructed from wooden panels and sheets of corrugated metal. The windows had been smashed, and the apertures were covered with plastic bags. Part of the tarpaulin roof was missing, and the front door had been separated from the hinges. Mysha pulled it aside so that they could enter, and once they were inside, she pulled it back into place.

Beatrix looked around the shack. It had been built right onto the ground, with no floor, and the sand was cold and yielding underfoot. Blankets and rugs were spread out to try and make things look more homely, but they only emphasised the spaces that were left uncovered. Blankets that had been hung from the ceiling broke the space into two distinct areas: one for sleeping and the other for cooking and eating. The walls were made of ill-fitted planks of wood, the gaps between them letting in shafts of light. There was a jerrycan of fresh water that must have been collected from a well, a small gas stove, a paraffin lamp, some sticks of furniture and a line that had been strung from one corner of the room to the other, bowing with the weight of damp clothing. There was a bucket in the corner. Beatrix guessed that was the toilet.

"Is this your home?"

"Yes," the girl said. "Your head," she added, as if keen to change the subject, embarrassed perhaps. She reached a cautious hand in the direction of the bloody wound on Beatrix's temple.

Beatrix caught her hand and smiled. "I'm fine," she said. "I'll just have a nice bruise to remind me what happened."

"You are bleeding. Here." She went to the sink, took a dishcloth and soaked it in water. Beatrix lowered herself to her haunches so that Mysha could dab the blood away. "Are you sure you are alright?"

"It's just a scratch. Thank you."

The girl rinsed the blood from the cloth and hung it out to dry. "Would you like something to drink?"

"That would be nice."

The girl went to a cupboard and filled a saucepan with cold water. She placed it on the small stove and set it to boil while she prepared the tea leaves and cardamom. Beatrix sensed that something was unsaid. The girl was putting on a brave face, but there was something that she wanted to talk about.

Beatrix would normally have thanked her and left. She should have done just that. There were things to do, and the world wasn't standing still. Duffy wasn't indulging himself with a hard luck story, she could be certain of that. He *must* have seen her, and now every second that passed meant that he was eroding the advantage that she had over him. There was nothing that could be done about that. There was no profit in her being found all the way out here, unprepared, unready. It made sense for her to hide out for an hour or two until she had found a way to get a message to Faulkner. Then she would bring the fight to him.

"Where are your parents?"

"I don't have any," she said as she worked.

"What do you mean?"

Beatrix heard the faintest quiver in her voice. "They are dead."

"What happened?"

"My father died during the war. He was a soldier. The Americans bombed his tank. There is a road from Basra that heads to Baghdad. A lot of traffic that day. Many tanks. The Americans sent bomb after bomb. Many men were killed. I was a baby. My mother told me what happened. I do not remember him."

"And your mother?"

"She was shot."

"By who?"

"The security men. She was one of the ones they killed. The shooting at the office of the oil company. Did you hear about that?"

"Yes, I did. A little."

"There was a big protest. Bigger than today. Angrier. Many people complaining that jobs were going to foreigners and not local people. My mother complained for my brother."

"Were you there, too?"

"At the back. I saw."

That was why she had been returning. She wanted justice, and there was no other means to get it for a twelve-year-old girl.

Until now, perhaps.

That was it. Beatrix realised why she wasn't able to leave. It was safest to stay; that was part of it, but it wasn't all of it. There was something of Isabella in the young Iraqi girl. The same age, give or take. The same stoicism. Abandoned, just the same. Her own sense of guilt, buried just beneath the surface, couldn't be ignored. She couldn't leave her now without knowing if she could help. Money, perhaps. She had plenty.

"You said you had a brother?"

"Yes."

"Where is he?"

"The security men arrested him. He wouldn't leave my mother when they told everyone to move away. They hit him in the head with their rifles and took him away."

"Do you know where he is?"

"I do not know for sure. There is a building where they say they keep their prisoners. Perhaps there."

"Has he been charged?"

"I do not know. I do not understand what is involved. He has done nothing wrong. I hope they will release him. But I have not seen him since they took him away."

Beatrix was humbled by the little girl's grace and composure. She had been orphaned, and now her brother had been arrested, too. There was no one to help her. How had she buried her mother? Had she been able to? How had she managed to do anything?

"Do you have any other relatives?"

"Not in Iraq. We have an aunt and uncle in Kuwait. But I have never met them."

She had been put through a terrible experience that would have crushed most people, and yet here she was, trying to maintain what was left of the family home, waiting patiently for her brother to be released. But what if he wasn't released? The riot would be characterised as inspired by insurgents. That would be the story that they would tell. And what if he was implicated in that? What if he met with an accident while in custody? What if he was disappeared? Juntas had been using those tactics to keep the people under the yoke for centuries.

"You said you were a journalist, Beatrix."

Beatrix regretted that she had lied to her now. "Yes," she said, because what else could she say? "That's right."

"Perhaps you could tell a story about what has happened?"

"To your brother?"

"Yes. Perhaps it would make a difference."

"Yes," she said. "Perhaps it would."

The girl smiled and exhaled, and Beatrix watched as the enforced maturity sloughed away and she saw her for exactly what she was: a twelve-year-old girl who was growing up too fast under the most awful circumstances. Beatrix thought again of Isabella, and the loss that she was going to have to face before the year was out. A loss on top of all the other losses. The thought brought the pain back to the surface in a sudden rush, and she couldn't suppress the wince.

"Are you alright?" Mysha said, hurrying over to her.

"Maybe he hit me harder than I thought he did." She braced against a chair and did not resist as the girl guided her down into it.

"You should rest, Beatrix."

"Maybe I should."

"It is getting late. Stay here tonight. I will tell you about my brother. For your story."

The hour was getting late, that was true. Beatrix thought about it. There was very little that she would be able to do this evening, and in any event, Duffy might have already started to look for her by now. Roadblocks were a possibility. Rolling patrols. Her earlier decision was right: it made sense for her to lie low for a few hours until the initial impetus waned. If it were her looking for him, she would scour the immediate area and then gradually widen the perimeter until it reached the city, and then she would search the hotels.

The risk of discovery was greatest now.

It was safer to stay where she was.

And it would give Faulkner a chance to make an assessment, too, and work out the safest way for her to return to the city.

And she felt so very, very tired.

"Thank you, Mysha. That's very kind. But I need to speak to my colleague. He will be worried about me. Do you have a telephone I could use?"

"Of course," Mysha said. "It was my mother's. There is some credit on it." She opened a box and took out an old-fashioned Nokia. She switched it on and handed it to Beatrix.

Beatrix had memorised Faulkner's number. "It's me," she said as soon as the call connected.

"What happened?"

Mysha surely wouldn't be able to speak English, but she spoke quietly and quickly, nonetheless. "A demonstration of how Manage Risk does its business."

"Are you alright?"

"I got cold-cocked, but I'll live. Where were you?"

"They moved me on. I doubled back, but they wouldn't let me get anywhere near you."

"It's fine, Faulkner. Relax. I'm fine."

"Did you get closer to Duffy?"

"Yes. It's him. He was there. Right in the middle of it. I think he saw me."

"Shit."

Mysha brought her another cup of tea.

"What do we do next?" Faulkner asked.

"If he did see me, he'll be looking for me now. The road back to the city won't be safe. I've got somewhere to stay tonight. I'm out of the way."

"And?"

"And I'll need you to come and pick me up. Tomorrow morning. Seven."

She told him where she was.

"Fine. And then?"

"I need you to arrange a call with Pope."

He hesitated. "Okay . . . you want to tell me what you want to speak to him about? Because I know he's going to ask."

"You need to tell him there's going to be a change of plan."

101

"We're still going to get Mackenzie West?"

"I promised Pope I would, and so we will."

"What about Duffy?"

"We're going to need him to help us do what I want to do."

"You think that's likely?"

"I can be persuasive."

———————

Mysha busied herself by the stove, coming over to check on Beatrix at regular intervals and bringing fresh cups of tea. Beatrix didn't have her bag with her, and the Zomorph was in it. The pain was bad, but she was going to have to go without her pills. She concentrated on her breathing, and after a while, the pain receded a little.

The shack grew dark as the hour drew on. Mysha lit the paraffin lamp and hung it from a hook on one of the joists that supported the ceiling. The light was warm and inviting, flickering against the blanketed walls. Beatrix drifted in and out of sleep until she became aware of pleasant aromas. Mysha brought her a tray of food. She had prepared *sabich*, pita stuffed with fried aubergine and hard-boiled eggs. There was also shawarma, a wrap made of shaved lamb and goat.

"Have you kept food for yourself?" Beatrix said as the girl passed the plate across to her.

"Yes, I have plenty," she said, although Beatrix knew that she was probably lying.

"Here," she said, tearing the shawarma and passing half back to her.

"No . . ."

"Eat it, Mysha."

The girl paused, but then did as she was told. She finished it quickly, betraying her hunger.

"Do you have a photograph of your brother?"

"For your story?"

"Yes."

"Of course."

She went over to a bag at the other side of the hut, and when she returned, she had a passport photo. She gave it to Beatrix. The young man in the photograph couldn't have been much older than twenty. He was handsome, with a clear and open face and thick, jet-black hair. His hazel eyes sparkled with life.

"What's his name?"

"His name is Faik. Faik al-Kaysi."

"And his age?"

"Nineteen."

"Do you mind if I borrow this?"

Her face flinched with reluctance.

"Don't worry. He can bring it back himself after I get him out."

"You can do that . . . ?"

"I'm going to try."

Mysha put her fingers to her cheek, and her lip quivered. "I . . ."

"It's alright, Mysha. I'm going to speak to some people I know. They will be able to help."

Her voice cracked a little. "Thank you."

She reached out and took the girl by the shoulder. "There's something else. My station pays for stories . . ."

"I don't want anything," she interrupted quickly.

"I would feel bad if I didn't pay you."

She was about to protest again, but she was stalled by Beatrix's raised hand. She put the other one into her pocket and took out two fifty-dollar bills. She pressed them into the girl's hand.

"Don't worry," she said. "I'll make sure you get your brother back again."

"Thank you," she sniffled, almost pitifully grateful.

Beatrix looked up at the wall opposite her. There were a dozen school achievement medals that had been clipped to the fabric covering, all in the name of Mysha al-Kaysi and all from at least three years ago.

"Those are very impressive," Beatrix said.

Mysha was busying herself with cleaning the stove. She looked up and looked over to where Beatrix was pointing. She smiled shyly. "It is nothing. Just school."

"Do you still go?"

"Not any more. I have to look after the house now that my . . ." She started to say "mother," then "brother," and then she stopped and looked down at the stove again. "It is alright. I was lucky to be able to go at all. Many of my friends cannot. They cannot read or write."

"What do you want to do when you're older?"

Mysha looked at her as if Beatrix was fooling with her. "When I am older? I will be a wife, if Allah is willing."

"You don't want to do something else? A career?"

"This is not America, Beatrix. That is not for me. I will be happy to have a husband and a family."

"And your brother wants to work on the oil field?"

"It is a good paying job. We do not have much. It would help." She looked reluctant as she said it.

"What do you think?"

"It is dangerous. Many men are injured. Many die. I would worry."

Beatrix finished the food and then helped to wash the dishes. The girl pulled a box away from the wall and took out blankets and a pillow. She arranged them in the centre of the makeshift room, layering the blankets to soften the rough contours of the bare earth. When she had finished, there were two separate beds. She indicated that Beatrix should lie down.

She did as she was told.

"Good night," the girl said.

She extinguished the paraffin lamp, and the shack fell dark.

"Good night."

Beatrix couldn't sleep.

She was in an unfamiliar place, in an unfriendly country. The silence was intermittent, disturbed by a loud and drunken argument from the next shack along, the misfiring of a car engine and, in the distant desert, the howling of wild dogs.

But the inability to rest was thanks to more than those distractions.

She closed her eyes again, but her mind was racing too fast and would not be still. She gave up and sat, removed the blankets and as quietly as she could, she stood up. Mysha was beside her, snoring very lightly, her breath going in and out with a light snuffle. Beatrix stepped over her legs and pulled aside the tarpaulin that covered the door. She went outside.

Something was different. Unusual. It was quiet now. The argument had subsided, the car had passed on and the dogs had either found something to eat or had moved away.

She looked up. The moon was shaded a burnt reddish-orange, the light reflecting through the smog from the burning gas and the sand in the air. It reminded her of a blood moon. Beatrix had seen one before, in Africa, so long ago that it seemed like another lifetime. There had been fresh blood on her hands then, the corpse of the Zimbabwean arms dealer still warm in the sand at her feet. He had dealt death and misery all around the continent, and he had, without doubt, warranted her attention. Beatrix had never given him a second thought, but now she found herself wondering about his situation: Had he had a wife, children, loved ones? Did that make any difference?

A blood moon.

How appropriate.

She sat in the sand and watched the sky for thirty minutes, the incremental progress of the red stain as it seemed to darken and swallowed the whole of the moon.

She reached into her pocket and took out the torn strip of photographs. She unfolded it and looked at her daughter and the way that she was looking at her. She touched her fingertips against her sweet face.

Her thoughts ran away with her. She was thinking about the decisions that she had made. Once Isabella had been returned to her care and could no longer be used against her, she had made the decision to wipe out those who had done her wrong.

To *extinguish* them.

But was it a decision? A decision required alternatives, different paths that could be taken in lieu of the one that she had chosen. Did she have a choice in any of this? Were there other paths? How much room was there for free will?

She had spent almost a decade nursing her grudges, dripping poison into the open wounds that had been inflicted by the five men and one woman who had found their way onto her list. The wound had festered and become septic. There had never been any chance for it to heal. After long enough, the need to avenge herself on them had become reflexive, as instinctive as the scratching of an itch.

She had never stopped to think about whether there was another course that she could take.

She stretched out her legs to ease the ache and considered. She could stop, she supposed, and ignore what had been done to her. Not forgive them, and never forget, but just let the hatred go and abandon her short future to fate. But too much had already happened for that to be possible. There *were* choices, but those choices had consequences, too. Her own decisions were one thing. She couldn't influence theirs. She could go back to the riad, but they would find her. She could flee and hide somewhere else, but they would find her there, too. Perhaps the cancer would finish her before they did, but that was no solace.

Because there was Isabella, too.

Control and the others knew that Beatrix was in the world now, looking for them; their names were on a list, all ready to be struck out. They would do everything they could to protect themselves. She knew Control. He would feel cornered and vulnerable, and the only possible response for a man like him would be to go on the attack. There would be no respite. No surcease. She could go dark again, and he wouldn't rest. He would be relentless, determined, and tear down the world until he found her. He had resources behind him that she couldn't hope to beat. If she delayed, she would lose all of her advantages. He would find her in the end, and when he did, there would be nothing that she could do.

She had to take the battle to him while she had the advantage. She would keep moving, perpetual motion, so that he could be kept off balance.

She looked at the photographs again.

She had her daughter to think about now.

She had no choice.

There were no alternatives.

She was set on a course that she could not change.

Immutable.

Indelible.

Unshakeable.

She had to follow it to its destination, whatever that was.

She looked up into the darkened vault of the sky again. The moon, plump and fat, was suspended above the rolling dunes, an orange counterpoint to the flames that burned on the horizon, the torches of fired gas. The crimson filter crept all the way across the silver disc, staining it all. Beatrix stood, brushing the sand from her legs. Her mind was clear now. She knew that she had no choice in any of this. Her fate was a focussed beam, from here to its vanishing point, that allowed no possibility of diversion. There was peace in that knowledge, and her mind, finally, was quietened.

She folded the strip of photographs along the crease and slipped it back into her pocket again.

She went back inside, fastened the tarpaulin behind her and returned to her bed. She was asleep within minutes.

Chapter Nineteen

The news that Ahmed was dead passed around the cell quickly, and then it was passed down the corridor to the other cells. It was adorned with new information, some of it true and plenty of it false, until it returned to their cell the next day so changed that it was difficult to know what to believe. The suggestion that he had suffered a heart attack was debunked, and now everyone believed the same thing: he had been tortured for his impertinence and had died during the ordeal.

That was probably true. The details didn't matter.

The temperature rose higher and higher until the atmosphere was feverish.

Faik withdrew to the back of the cell. There was always violence just beneath the surface, but now it seemed dangerously close and ready to catch light. He didn't want to be anywhere near the front when it started.

He didn't have long to wait.

The guard with the shotgun went off shift, to be replaced by a man Faik recognised. No one knew his name, but since he had a cruel, braying laugh, he had quickly become known as *hîmaar*, or Donkey. He was a regular, and renowned for his sadism. He had spat into Faik's bowl of rice on his first day inside, and there were stories of his particularly enthusiastic participation in the six-on-one beatings that the guards used to punish those inmates who had done something that they found objectionable. He was also a heavy drinker, and Faik had noticed that he was often drunk while he was on shift. Tonight, Donkey was sweating heavily and he reeked of alcohol again; perhaps that was why he misread the atmosphere.

One of the inmates stood up and walked over to the door. He was a young man called Abdul, just a little older than Faik, and of a similarly slight build. He would not have been the sort to arouse wariness or suspicion.

He called Donkey to come over.

The man swore in irritation, but raised himself from the chair and, with his shotgun held loosely at his side, came closer to the bars of the cell.

"What?"

Abdul grabbed Donkey by the collar of his shirt and yanked hard, pulling him onto the bars. His head bounced off the metal, and he grunted in pain and surprise. A second inmate, Abdul's older brother Tarik, leapt to his feet and reached through to grab the guard's flailing left arm, pulling hard so that he was trapped against the bars. He dropped the shotgun and shouted in sudden fear, but the other guards were in the guardhouse with a crate of Asrihah *arak* and oblivious to what was going on outside. Donkey kept his keys on a loop that hung from his belt, right next to his revolver. Abdul tore the keys from the belt and Tarik reached for the revolver. Donkey fought desperately, punching through the bars with his right fist and managing to hold him off.

But now Abdul had the cell door open.

"Come on!" he yelled.

Donkey freed his arm and staggered away from the bars. He thought about the shotgun on the floor, saw the open gate and the men who were pouring out of it, and fled.

Tarik hurried outside and took the shotgun.

The other prisoners hurried to get out.

Faik stayed at the back. He felt sick with fright. He was unable to move.

The engineer started for the door, paused, looked back at him and then pushed through the scramble until he was close enough to reach down and pull him up.

"Come on," he said, urgently, his eyes flashing. "You can't stay here. We have to go."

"They'll shoot us."

"And what will they do if we stay?"

Faik looked into his face and saw resolution. He allowed himself to be pulled up and to the open door and out into the corridor beyond.

———

They tried to open the other cells first, but Donkey's key didn't work in all of them. They opened three, and so there were a hundred or so prisoners who made it out. That was still more than enough to overpower the drunken guards. They swarmed into the room where they were drinking their *arak* and piled onto them, burying them under a weight of numbers and raining a brutal shower of kicks and punches down onto them until all were either dead or unconscious. They took their revolvers and another shotgun and pressed buttons until they had unlocked the gate to the canteen. They surged inside, roaring with pent-up fury, turning over tables and throwing chairs. A fire extinguisher was torn from the wall and crashed down again and again on the toughened glass in the door that opened out onto the exercise yard.

Faik was jostled into the middle of the mêlée as the door was battered open and the prisoners spilled out into the cool night air. They had exited into the exercise yard. The dusty surface looked lunar in the illumination of the prison's lighting, and the first few men started to sprint across the fifty feet of open space to the nearest wall.

Faik cowered in the lee of the building.

This all felt horribly dangerous.

"Come on," the engineer urged him. "There is a weakness in the fence. Over there, it is possible to open it. I have seen. Come on!"

He ran, and Faik followed, slowly at first and then faster.

Maybe he could get out.

Maybe he could get back to Mysha.

Maybe they could leave town.

Maybe . . .

There came a crack that echoed out across the wide space.

There were several prisoners ahead of them, heading for the same weakness that the engineer had identified.

Faik watched in horror as the head of the man farthest from them jerked back at him, a pink mist spraying out. His momentum carried him forward for another step, but then he toppled backwards, landing with a heavy thud on his shoulder blades.

There came another, echoing report.

The second man of the pair was drilled through the neck. He stumbled onwards for a handful of paces, turning back to them with his hands clasped around his throat, before he slumped to his knees and then keeled over onto his side.

Faik stopped. He looked up at the guard tower that overlooked the main gate. One of the sentries was turned in their direction. He had braced his left forearm on the timber balustrade, the stock of his sniper rifle nestled tight between his sternum and his chin. He was gently obscured by a pall of grey smoke that had issued from the muzzle of the long gun, quickly dissipating into the night.

The engineer stopped, too.

There was a third sharp pop, and the engineer jerked from the middle. The shot turned him around, and he stumbled towards Faik, a look of incomprehension on his face. A dot of red appeared on his orange jumpsuit and then burgeoned, the edges pushing outwards until it bloomed wider than the span of the hands he pressed against it. He moaned, his eyes rolled back into his head and he toppled down onto his face like a felled tree.

Faik dropped to the ground and covered his head with his arms. He closed his eyes and waited.

Chapter Twenty

Bryan Duffy dropped the unconscious body of the protester in the shaded courtyard between the administrative buildings where Manage Risk planned its work in Energy City. There were a dozen men and a few women there already, all of them recovering from their forcible removal from the area near the gates. Duffy's man had been jostled into him amid the crush, and he had pistol-whipped him across the forehead, knocking him out. He prodded him with the toe of his steel-capped boot and flipped him over onto his back. Blood was running freely from the deep gash in his scalp, and his head lolled on floppy muscles. The team would wait until they were recovered and then ship them back to the city. There would be charges for vandalism and public disorder, a quick trial and a long stay in the new al-Mina prison.

Duffy was responsible for security at Energy City. It was a demanding job, but that was why the company had been able to charge ten million a year to keep the place safe. Duffy had shares in Manage Risk, and it was in his best interests to project the right image. Tough. Ruthless. No pity for anyone who threatened the status quo. He took his job seriously, and he was good at it.

They had quelled the riot before it could get started, but he was not happy as he pushed open the swing door into the air-conditioned oasis that was the hub of the operation. He was not happy at all.

"McNulty," he said.

"Yes, boss?"

"I need you to put a team together."

"For what?"

"I thought I saw someone today," he said absently. "In the crowd."

"Someone?"

He waved a hand. "Someone I used to work with. A long time ago. I haven't seen her for a while."

He took out his phone, opened his photos and selected the one that he wanted. It was ten years old, the most recent one their contact in the Group had been able to find. The picture was of a smiling Beatrix Rose in the Sahara Desert with an officer from the Moroccan army who stood alongside her. She had long, straight, blonde hair; beautifully crafted features; porcelain skin; and a slender figure. Her eyes were an icy blue, the bluest that he had ever seen.

He slid the phone across the desk, and McNulty looked at the picture. "Good-looking woman," he said with leering grin. "If it were me, I'd be looking for her, too."

"No," he said. "Trust me, you wouldn't."

Duffy looked at the photograph again. He remembered how attractive Beatrix had been.

Had he seen her?

If it wasn't her, it was someone who looked very much like her.

Normally, he would have passed it off as a mistake or a trick of the light. But he knew what had happened to Oliver Spenser and Joshua Joyce. And then, just the day after he had spoken to her, someone had put a bomb under Lydia Chisholm's car and detonated it with her inside. It was difficult to look at the trail of dead and not see the pattern.

Number Five: Chisholm.

Number Eight: Spenser.

Number Ten: Joyce.

He had been Number Eleven on that day, nearly a decade ago, when Beatrix Rose's family had been torn away from her.

If it was her and she had a list, his name was definitely on it.

"Is it going to be a problem, skip?"

"I don't know," Duffy said, although he did.

If it was Beatrix Rose, "problem" didn't even get *close*.

Chapter Twenty-One

Beatrix awoke with the dawn. The sunlight suffused the material that was hung on the walls, the fabric rippling gently in the early morning breeze that was blowing off the desert. She looked up at the ceiling, where the joists met in the middle, and remembered where she was. She had fallen quickly into a deep and dreamless sleep. The night had been cold, and she noticed with a pang, the girl had covered her with another blanket. She pressed against the ground with her right arm and raised herself to a sitting position. Mysha wasn't there.

The pain returned as soon as she stood, falling over her as if it had just been waiting for the moment when she had almost forgotten about it. She fought against nausea and then the dizziness that followed in its wake as she stood. She wobbled and then shambled to the shack's single rickety wooden chair. She fell down into it and was still there, breathing deeply, eyes closed, when Mysha yanked aside the tarpaulin and came inside. Her face fell when she saw Beatrix.

"Are you unwell?"

"I got up a little too fast. I'm fine."

The girl was carrying the jerrycan, and it sloshed with water as she set it down. She must have been to the well. She lit the stove, filled the saucepan and set it to boil.

"Did you sleep well?"

"I did. Thank you."

Mysha prepared the spiced cardamom tea and brought Beatrix a cup. She sipped it, the spices chasing away the metallic aftertaste of the vomit that had crept up from her gullet.

"Where is the well?"

"The other village."

"How far?"

"Two miles, there and back."

"What time did you wake?"

"I get up at four," she said. "I always have things to do."

They both heard the single blast of a car's horn from outside. Beatrix looked at her watch. It was seven, the time that she had arranged with Faulkner.

Beatrix finished the tea and gingerly levered herself upright.

"Are you leaving now?"

"Yes. I expect that's my friend."

Beatrix collected her jacket and her Oakleys and checked her reflection in the mirror that was hanging next to the door. There was a picture of a man and a woman tucked into the brass frame. Mysha's parents. There was a *hijab* on a hook next to the mirror. It must have belonged to Mysha's mother.

"Could I borrow this?" she asked.

"Yes," the girl said with a nod.

Beatrix wrapped it around her head.

"Thank you," Beatrix said. "And thank you for the tea."

She stooped to hug the girl.

She still had her clasped in an embrace as she reached her right hand back into her pocket and took out the rest of the notes that she had brought with her. There were five or six hundred dollars in all, Beatrix couldn't remember how much exactly. She flicked the tight roll with her index finger and propelled it onto the chair in which she had been sitting. It bumped once, twice, and settled against the cushion. Mysha was still in her embrace and didn't notice. Beatrix put her hands on the girl's shoulders and moved her a step backwards.

"If I get your brother, you have to promise me something."

"Yes?"

"Stay away from the protest. It isn't safe. Do you promise?"

"Yes," she said. "I promise." She looked up at her with hopeful eyes. "When will you be able to find Faik?"

"I'm going to start right away."

Chapter Twenty-Two

Duffy shut the door to his office and opened the encrypted videoconferencing app on his laptop. There was a delay of a few seconds as the connection was made, and then the screen showed the inside of another office, bright sunshine streaming through an open window. He waited for moment, listening to the sound of conversation off-camera, until the man he wanted to speak to sat down at the chair in front of the camera. He was a little plump, with bushy eyebrows that topped eyes that seemed caught in a perpetual glower. His face was lined and worn, and the beard that he wore was shot through with more grey than Duffy could remember. He did not know the man's real name. None of them did. His designation within Group Fifteen had always been Control, and it had stayed the same despite the fact that he had fled his previous employment in disgrace.

They all had that much in common, at least.

"Yes?" he said curtly. There was something of the public school-master in the way he spoke to his agents. He was supercilious, abrupt and short of patience. Duffy did not like him, but he did respect him. He was an operator of the highest order, a master strategist, and he had connections throughout the world. Colonels and admirals, spies and spymasters, they all answered his calls.

Duffy was not afraid of many people.

Control was different.

He spoke carefully. "We may have a problem."

"I hope not," Control said irritably. "We're coming up to renewal. That nonsense with the protesters hasn't gone down well with the Iraqis. We cannot afford to have anything else like that."

"I know," he said, taking a deep breath. "That is under control, I told you."

"You said that before."

"It was then, and it is now. That's not why we need to speak. It's something else."

Worse than that.

"Out with it."

"It's Rose."

Even with the buffering on the call, it was obvious that this had rattled Control. "Why do you say that?"

"Because I think I saw her."

"Where?"

"There was another protest yesterday. Not as bad as before; we kept it under wraps, but I saw someone in the crowd. It might have been her."

"You *think*? It *might*? You need to be sure."

"I'm not sure. I know I've been thinking about it a lot since we talked about her, about Spenser and Chisholm and Joyce, and I know it's possible I'm seeing things when there's nothing to see. But I'm pretty sure I saw a Western woman, medium height, slender build. Blonde hair."

"You *think*?" Control said again.

"There was another sighting. One of our patrols, just outside the facility—they pulled over an SUV with a blonde woman inside.

She had papers for onward travel, but they had been faked. She said she was a journalist. BBC."

"And?"

"And so I checked with them. They don't have anyone in Basra. They haven't had anyone here for a month. I showed the men who pulled the SUV her picture. And they think . . ."

"I need something better than that!" he snapped.

"And they think, high probability, that it's her."

Control glared into the camera. "I'm not going to pull you out of there on the basis of that. It's not enough."

"I didn't say I wanted you to pull me out."

"So why are you bothering me with this?"

Because you asked.

Because you need to know, too.

Because if she crosses a line through my name, you might be next.

Duffy bit his lip. Control's temper had been much worse since Milton and Rose had wiped out the team in Russia and forced him into hiding. That was understandable enough. If Rose was working her way through a Kill List, then his name was right at the top.

"Look, I just wanted you to know," he said. "If it is her, at least I'm forewarned. *We're* forewarned. I'm not going anywhere. She won't be able to get the jump on me like she did with Joyce. We're looking for *her* now. The shoe is on the other foot. We know she's coming."

"Have you started?"

"I've got men at the hotels. We'll try them all. She has to be staying somewhere."

"It won't be as easy as that. She was good, Duffy. The best until John Milton. Maybe even better than him."

And she's just one person in a place that we control, Duffy thought. *A place we have flooded with soldiers. And we know she's coming. It doesn't matter how good she is.*

He paused. "Did you find anything out about where she went after Somalia?"

Control frowned. "Only two leads. Someone who looks very like her flew out of Kenya. There were only a handful of flights out that day. Fuel spill on the taxiway shut the airport down. Casablanca or Durban look like possibilities. We've got men looking into it."

Duffy nodded and cracked his knuckles. "That's all I had for you, sir. Thank you."

"Keep me posted."

Control ended the call.

Duffy stood and collected his holstered pistol from the back of his chair. He put it on.

Time to go to work.

⌣───⌣

Duffy and McNulty drew up at the hotel. They were in an unmarked Land Rover, with the four men that they had brought along for the job in another Land Rover behind them. Each man was armed with a semi-automatic, and McNulty had a Remington Model 870 Pump in a sports bag that was stowed in the back.

Duffy picked up the handheld radio and thumbed the channel open. "Wide awake, boys," he said. "The target is a serious player. Eyes open."

"How serious?" McNulty said beside him.

"You don't want to know."

Duffy got out of the Land Rover and made his way to the hotel's entrance. It was plush, at least as far as Basra went, and he was a little surprised that Beatrix Rose would have considered this a suitable place to stay. It was hardly low-key, for one. It would have been more usual for a member of the Group to find somewhere deep in the city, somewhere that no self-respecting tourist would ever consider, in order to rise out of the background, do the job and then fall back out of sight once again. But his contact in the local police had reported that a foreigner who matched Rose's description had checked in to the hotel. She was a striking woman, especially here. There couldn't be many like her in a city like this. It was a good lead, the best that they had received. They had to check it out.

His contact from the Basra police department was waiting in the lobby with two of his colleagues. The man was called Tariq, and he was the most crooked man that Duffy had ever met.

"Did you get it?" Duffy asked.

"I did." He held up a sheet of paper. "A judicial search order."

"Any trouble?"

Tariq smiled his brightest, most avaricious smile. "No trouble, Mr Duffy. You have something for me?"

"Sure." He handed over an envelope. "Five hundred dollars for you and your friends. Knock yourselves out."

"We must come up with you. We will open the door, and then if she is there, and you happen to go inside?" He spread his hands wide. "What can we do?"

The blonde woman and her companion had checked into adjoining rooms on the fourth floor. Duffy left one of his men in the lobby and sent another two up the stairs. The Iraqi police went up in the first lift, and Duffy, McNulty and the fourth operative took the second.

"Think she's here?" McNulty asked him as the lift ascended.

"I don't know." He slipped his hand inside his jacket and drew out the Walther PPK that he had holstered beneath his arm. "Best to assume that she is."

The fourth-floor lobby was empty. The two operatives who had taken the stairs appeared, and Duffy told them to stand guard. Tariq told his two colleagues to do the same and set off down the corridor, stopping outside room 415.

Duffy followed. McNulty was behind him, the Remington held in both hands.

Tariq took the key card that he had requisitioned at reception and, after checking that Duffy was ready, slipped it into the slot.

The lock changed from red to green, and the door clicked open a fraction.

"Ready?" Duffy asked McNulty and the other operative.

Both men raised their weapons and nodded that they were.

Duffy kicked the door open.

He went inside, nerves afire, clearing the en-suite bathroom and then the bedroom beyond.

Empty.

It was a decent enough room; clothes lay scattered across the bed. He picked up a white T-shirt. There was a towel on the floor, still damp.

"She's been here," he said. "Not long ago."

McNulty came out of the bathroom. "Shower's only just been used," he said.

"*Dammit.*"

"What do you want me to do?"

"Go down to the lobby. Close the hotel down and call for backup. No one goes in or comes out. She might still be in the building."

"Will do."

McNulty and Tariq left him alone.

There was a box of bullets on the bed. Nine-millimetre hollow points. He picked up the box. It was empty.

It was her. She had been here. They had missed her by a matter of minutes.

This had been his chance. His best and only chance. There had only been one opportunity, and it had passed. She knew, for sure, that they were onto her now. She would be a ghost. They wouldn't see her again until she decided to come for them.

For him.

Chapter Twenty-Three

Faik had been alone for almost twenty-four hours. They had brought him to the punishment wing after the riot had been pitilessly quelled. Solitary confinement. He had only seen fleeting glimpses of his fellow inmates as they returned from interrogations, and he had heard the sound of prisoners moaning in their cells after heavy-handed beatings. The long hours of the night had been filled with desperation and restlessness, and it had continued into the day. He had no idea what was planned for him, and into that void came doubt and terror. His sleep was haunted by awful dreams that he couldn't make stop.

The isolation cell was tiny. He could touch the walls with both hands when he stretched out his arms. There was a bucket for a toilet, no chair and nothing to sleep on save the cold, hard, concrete floor. He had been given no food or drink, and the cell was so stiflingly hot that he felt woozy.

A door opened and closed, and he heard footsteps approach from down the corridor. His stomach clenched. Part of him willed the footsteps to continue to another cell. The other part wanted them to stop and his door to be unlocked and opened so that he might have fresh air and water.

A key was inserted into the lock and turned. The door opened.

It was Donkey, with two other guards behind him.

There was no water and no food.

He was carrying a hood and a pair of handcuffs. The hood was stained with little smudges and smears of brown.

Donkey's expression was gleeful.

Faik shrank away, but there was nowhere for him to go.

The guards crowded into the cell.

Donkey pressed him back against the wall.

"It is time for a little chat," he said.

The two guards took his arms and restrained him as Donkey pulled the hood over his head. It was made from burlap, coarse against his skin. Little pinpricks of light hovered before his eyes. They fastened it with a drawstring, yanking it so hard that it bit into his throat.

Something heavy smacked into his face, his chin, and the pinpricks of light were extinguished.

———

He was too woozy to pay much attention to where he was being taken. Two of the guards were on either side of him, dragging him down the corridor, the rubber soles of his sandals squealing against the linoleum. A door was opened and he was thrown inside. His hands had been cuffed, and he landed heavily, the resounding impact against his chin snuffing out the consciousness that had started to return.

Minutes passed.

The hood was yanked away without warning.

Bright, artificial lights.

Starbursts exploded in his eyes.

He squeezed them shut.

Strong hands scooped beneath his shoulders and hauled him to his feet. He lolled helplessly as his arms were held out, cold steel bracelets snapping around his wrists. His arms were released, and there was a clank as the chains to which the cuffs were fastened took his weight.

"Wake up."

His head drooped loosely, his chin against his chest.

"Wake up, you son of a whore."

He gasped as a pail of cold water was upturned over his head. The shock ousted the last wisps of his stupor, and his eyes flicked open.

He was in the same interrogation room as before. The hose had been curled in the corner next to a sodden blanket. He was suspended from two chains which ran up to pulleys fixed into the ceiling. The guards held a chain each and they pulled down hard, jerking his arms straight up into the air, lifting him so that his toes just barely scraped against the floor. His sandals slipped off his feet. The muscles in his shoulders and the tops of his arms protested from the sudden effort of bearing his weight.

There was no camera this time. The tripod was still there, but it was empty.

Two powerful lights burned into his face.

Donkey was in front of him.

Faik still felt giddy, his sight distorted, double vision that made everything look blurred and ghostly.

"You are a terrorist," Donkey said to him.

Faik mumbled a denial.

"What?"

Faik mumbled again.

"I can't hear you."

"I am . . . not . . ."

"You organised the riot, did you not?"

"No . . . I . . ."

"*You* persuaded the others to break out of the cell. *You* attacked the guards. *You* murdered them, Faik. Didn't you?"

"No . . ."

"You are a terrorist. You are part of the Promised Day Brigade."

"No . . ."

"You know that dog Muqtada al-Sadr, do you not? You know that son of a cur."

"I do not . . ."

Donkey walked across to the other side of the room. Faik followed him with his eyes, watched as he bent down to a table that held a jumble of tools and other objects that he did not immediately recognise. He picked up an oblong object that looked as if it was heavy. Cables dangled from the object. The cables ended in tarnished crocodile clips. It was a battery.

"No," Faik begged as Donkey brought it over to him. "No, please, I haven't done anything wrong."

"They always say that," the man said. "But I get them to sing a different song."

Donkey nodded, and the guard to Faik's left reached across and tore open the jumpsuit, yanking it all the way down to his waist.

"Please," Faik begged. He pulled at the cuffs, but all that achieved was to swing him gently forward and back. His toes scraped along the concrete and then his momentum swung him forward and he dangled there. His muscles screamed from the strain.

"Do you think I am sadistic?"

Donkey rested the battery on the floor and held up the crocodile clips.

Faik tried to swing away from him. He could not.

"You would be right. I am sadistic. It is my only pleasure in this hellhole."

Faik struggled again. It was futile. Donkey reached over with his right hand and held him by the hip, deadening the impetus, holding him still.

"Let me tell you something," he said. "I will share some information with you. I am going to get you to confess to everything, but only because it pleases me that I can. There was a trial this morning. You were convicted of murdering three guards. There is no right of appeal to this conviction. It is binding. It cannot be changed. Do you know what that means?"

"I did not . . ."

Sneering, Donkey reached up with his left hand and gripped Faik's face. He squeezed his fingers, pushing his cheeks together so that he could only murmur and mumble.

"You can say what you want. You can deny everything, but it does not matter. Confess to everything, and it won't matter. You have been convicted of murder and treason. You, and all the others. You have been sentenced to death."

Chapter Twenty-Four

B eatrix had been in her room when she had heard the men
outside. She had showered, changed, and prepared her
weapons, and then she heard the lift and the men getting
out of it. There was an interconnecting door between her room and
Faulkner's, and she had very quietly opened it and slipped through.
Beatrix and Faulkner had waited quietly, her FN F2000 assault rifle
aimed at the door in anticipation of it opening. It hadn't.

The men had burst into her room instead, and that had given
Beatrix and Faulkner the moment that they needed.

They had hurried down the corridor, away from the men in the
lobby, and disappeared down the outside fire escape.

They ran across the parched gardens to Faulkner's Freelander.
Beatrix dumped the kit in the back.

"They're onto us," he said when he had slid inside next to her.

"We need to be careful from now."

"We could have taken him there."

"Maybe, maybe not. There were a lot of them. It would have
been messy."

"But . . ."

"I want him alive."

"Why?"

"Because we still need him. We don't know where West is. He does. And I have another use for him."

"And are you going to share that with me?"

"We're getting a man out of custody."

"I know," he said impatiently. "Mackenzie West."

"Someone else, too."

Faulkner frowned. "Alright. Humour me. Who?"

"His name is Faik. He's the brother of someone I met yesterday. But she didn't know where he was, other than that Manage Risk had him. Duffy will be able to help us find him."

"And then?"

"Yes," she said. "And then, that's that."

There was nothing else to say about that.

"Where are we going now?"

"I need you to find somewhere we can stay. It needs to be quiet. Out of the way. An abandoned building, somewhere we won't be disturbed."

"Okay. Fine. And you?"

"I'm going to tail him."

"He'll see you."

She reached into the kit bag and took out the *hijab* that she had borrowed from Mysha. She quickly pulled it over her head and arranged it so that it fell comfortably to her shoulders. "I don't think so," she said.

She got into the driver's seat.

"I'll call you."

She drove the Freelander out of the car park and placed it in a position away from the hotel and yet still close enough that she had a decent view of the entrance. Two cars pulled up and disgorged half a dozen men, all obviously ex-military and all, she guessed, in the employ of Manage Risk. Four police cars followed soon after, and between them, the hotel was quickly locked down. The Freelander was parked in an unobtrusive spot, and she was able to loiter there without attracting attention.

She waited fifteen minutes until Duffy came out, lighting a cigarette and talking to another man and one of the Basra police. He looked agitated, gesticulating angrily as he spoke.

He had a reason to be agitated.

He went back inside, but, after an additional ten minutes, he returned and got into one of the Manage Risk Land Rovers, negotiated the security measures and set off into the streets beyond.

Beatrix followed him north.

The damage wrought by the war had gone unrepaired. Street lights had been bent at unnatural angles by tanks. A deep crater in the road evidenced an IED. Several of the buildings in the street had gaps in the middle of them, neat surgical excisions where laser-guided munitions had carved them out, leaving tangled girders and piles of debris. Strangely, the blasts had spared the neighbouring properties.

They passed into an area of office buildings, and Duffy pulled over and parked next to one of them. It was four storeys tall and, compared to the dilapidated state of the building stock in the area, reasonably well maintained. Beatrix looked out as she passed him. The building bore a sign with the Roman insignia of the Manage Risk logo.

She drove a little farther and then turned the SUV around and drove back. She passed the office and parked fifty yards farther down the road. Making sure that the *hijab* was properly obscuring her face, she set off back towards the office.

She looked left and right. She passed an Iraqi in a cheap, shiny suit.

There was a small group of people sitting in a shaded bowyer, eating sandwiches. None of them paid her any heed.

As she closed in on the office, the front doors opened, and a tall, brawny military type stepped out. He cursed as the heat washed over him, shook his head in disbelief at how a place could be as hot as this and walked straight at her. He gazed in her direction, but looked right through her. The *hijab* made her almost invisible.

She slowed as she reached Duffy's vehicle. She reached into her pocket, took out the GPS tracker and slapped it so that it fastened to the chassis of the Land Rover above the wheel, obscured by the wheel arch.

She went back to the Freelander.

She waited.

⁓

Duffy drummed his fingers on the desk as the encryption software exchanged handshakes with the server in America. Control was at his desk when the connection was made.

"Duffy," he said. "What is it?"

"She's here. We were checking a lead. Western woman who might've matched her description had checked into the International. We went up to the room. It was her, alright. We'd just missed her."

"Alright. It goes without saying, but I'll say it anyway: be careful. She got up close to Spenser and Joyce and close enough to Chisholm. Expect something like that. I doubt she'll do it from a distance. You'd already be dead if that was good enough for her."

"So I have to look over my shoulder."

"Yes."

"How long do I have to do that for?"

"Just a few days. I'm sending Connor English to you. He has a team. Our best men. He's been preparing them for the last two weeks. They'll fly out tonight and be with you tomorrow. And then you can take the fight to her."

"Fine," he sighed.

"Don't fuck this up, Duffy. She's more dangerous when she's in the shadows. You've flushed her out. Stay alive long enough for English to get to you. Then it's your turn to have some fun."

Beatrix waited. Duffy was in the building for thirty minutes, and when he stepped outside again, he was wearing a dark and troubled frown. He got back into his Land Rover and drove away, following a route that took him farther to the north.

Beatrix settled a few car lengths behind him and took the smartphone from her pocket. She had already preprogrammed the number for the tracker, and she texted it. The unit texted back almost at once with its latitude and longitude, its speed and a link to a Google map. She opened the link and, after a moment, saw the tracker's position illuminated by a blue dot and her own by a red dot.

Everything was working as it should.

She stowed the phone in her pocket and settled in behind him.

She followed for twenty minutes. Duffy turned off the freeway and into an upscale residential neighbourhood. The farther he drove, the better the surrounding neighbourhoods became. The damage had been repaired, the roads resurfaced and the houses on either side of the street were newer and in bigger plots. The gardens were well irrigated, with lush green lawns and healthy palm trees despite the furnace-like sun that scorched down from above. *Oil money*, she thought. It was obvious.

He slowed and paused at the entrance to a gated compound.

Beatrix slowed, too, as much as she dared, and carried out a spot assessment.

The compound was surrounded by a ten-foot-high stone wall topped with razor wire. There were CCTV cameras spaced at regular intervals around the perimeter. The thick iron gate slid open and closed on a grooved track that was cut into the asphalt. The gate was guarded by two armed men.

She drove another twenty seconds up the road, turned, and then turned back. She studied the guards. They looked like soldiers. Each toted a Heckler & Koch MP-5. As she passed them, she noticed the Manage Risk logo on the sleeves of their black uniforms.

She shifted up to second and accelerated gently away. It would be difficult to get to Duffy at home.

She had another way.

Chapter Twenty-Five

It was nine in the morning the following day. Beatrix and Faulkner were laid up in the Freelander outside the compound where Duffy lived. Beatrix was watching the guards through the windows of the SUV. They were smart and alert, too wise to the risks of guarding high-value targets in a place like Basra to take their eyes off the ball, even for a moment. A direct attack could only lead to bloodshed, and she didn't want that. Not yet.

Faulkner had his smartphone in hand. He had called Pope overnight with a request for details on Mrs Sascha Duffy. Pope had passed the query on to the spooks at GCHQ, and they had assigned it with urgent tasking. The vast amount of data that they scraped from the internet was poured into endless data farms, but their automated scripts had interrogated those servers at lightning speed until they found what they were looking for.

A number had been texted to Faulkner and was waiting for him when he awoke.

"Ready?"

"Do it."

Faulkner dialled the number.

The call rang twice and then connected. Faulkner had it on the speakerphone.

"Hello?"

"Is this Sascha Duffy?" Faulkner said.

"Yes. Who is this?"

"My name is Doctor Miles Farrow. I'm calling from the al-Jamhouroua Hospital in Basra. It's about your husband."

"Bryan?"

"Yes, madam."

"Oh my goodness. Is he alright?"

"I'm afraid he's been quite badly hurt, Mrs Duffy. I don't know if you've seen the news today, but there was a bomb . . ."

"Badly hurt? What does that mean?"

"He's unconscious. We don't think he's in immediate danger, but you should probably come to the hospital as soon as you can. Do you know where we are?"

"Yes, I was there a month ago. A friend . . . oh, my goodness. I'll come right away. Which ward is he in?"

"He's in ICU, madam."

"Thank you."

Sascha Duffy rang off.

They waited. All they needed to do was to get her out of the gated compound, away from the security.

It didn't take long.

Sascha hurried out the front door and got into the Audi TT that was parked on the drive. Beatrix had wondered whether she would usually travel with a guard, but if she did, she was in too much of a hurry today to worry about it. She reversed off the drive and sped up to the lodge with the armed guards inside. She exchanged a quick few words, the gate slid to the side and she accelerated quickly away.

Faulkner pulled into the traffic behind her. They headed to the middle of town and the al-Jamhouroua hospital.

"She's going to come off here," Beatrix said, pointing to the slip road that fed off the main route.

Faulkner fed revs to the engine and picked up speed.

Sascha Duffy stopped at a red light that filtered traffic onto a roundabout. She was first at the light, and they were second. There was no one behind them. It was perfect.

Faulkner drew up to a stop behind the Audi.

Beatrix opened the door, got out and, drawing her Sig, jogged up to the passenger side door. She knew that it would be locked—that was *de rigeur* for a Western woman driving around Basra on her own—but that was not a problem. She used the butt of the pistol to smash the glass, reached in and opened the door from the inside and got in.

Sascha Duffy screamed and fumbled the car into first gear. Beatrix reached across and laid her right hand across Sascha's hand on the gearstick.

"Relax," she said. "I'm not going to hurt you. Your husband is fine." She laid the Sig on her lap, drawing the woman's eyes to it. "But I need you to come with me."

———

They waited until the GPS tracker on Duffy's car was on the move and then set off. Faulkner was in the Freelander and Beatrix was driving Sascha Duffy's Audi. Sascha was in the back, her hands fastened behind her back with cable ties.

Duffy had been at the Rumaila complex all day and into the night, and now he was coming back into Basra. That was ideal for what they had in mind. The road passed through the occasional village and shanty, but for the most part, it sliced through barren desert. It was a sixty-minute drive. There would be plenty of opportunities to do what had to be done.

They hurried out of the city, skirting Zubayr and finding a quiet spot on the road to the north of the Al Mufrash airstrip. The road here followed the route of a dried-out wadi, dipping down into a depression so that the sides rose up four or five feet. It was a natural choke point that would be impossible to evade without backing up.

Faulkner drove on for thirty seconds before running off-road and parked the Freelander behind a grove of palm trees that would hide it from traffic approaching from the southwest.

Beatrix drove around a curve that would hide the Audi until the last possible minute.

They waited. The sky was dark, the stars scattered like diamonds across velvet. The horizon was lightened by the flames from the oilfields, and the sound of machinery was audible from miles away.

She saw a pair of headlights in the distance, heading right at them. She took out her phone and texted the tracker.

It pinged back its response.

A blue dot closing in on her red dot.

Duffy.

She drove the Audi into the middle of the road, leaving it with no room to pass on either side.

She went to the back of the SUV, opened it, hauled Sascha Duffy out and took her around to the side of the car that would face approaching traffic.

"Wait here," she said. "It's nearly over now."

"What are you doing?"

"Wait."

She went back to the car and took out the FN F2000 assault rifle.

Duffy's Jeep Grand Cherokee bounced down into the dip, the headlights illuminating the walls of the wadi as it proceeded around the gentle curve.

Faulkner gunned the Freelander's engine and the SUV shot forward, blocking the way back and sealing Duffy inside.

Duffy exited the corner. The headlights shone over them: Beatrix, with the assault rifle cradled in her arms; his wife, averting her eyes from the glare of the lamps. Duffy hit the brakes and skidded to a stop. He reversed, the tyres chewing gravel as he tried to back away at speed.

The rifle was a bulky bullpup, chambered in 5.56 NATO. She nestled the stock into her shoulder and aimed, squeezing the trigger and sending a volley of bullets into the Grand Cherokee. The headlights shattered, the hood was torn up and both front tyres were shredded. The wheels sank down to the rims and carved tracks through the sand as the rear wheels dragged the disabled Jeep backwards. Beatrix aimed again and sent a volley through the windscreen. The glass crashed out of the frame, and rounds punched up and out of the roof.

Faulkner was out of the Freelander and approached the beached Jeep with his pistol raised. He fired, taking out the rear tyres and then the rear windscreen.

They both stopped firing.

Beatrix walked to the Jeep, the FN F2000 aimed straight at Duffy and her finger on the trigger.

"Get out!" Beatrix yelled over the sound of the still-straining engine.

The diesel revved again.

She stitched a jagged pattern of bullets into the hood for a second time.

"Get out, Duffy. I'll shoot your wife if you don't. And then I'll shoot you."

The engine quietened and then stopped.

The driver's side door opened and Duffy carefully stepped out.

"Hands behind your back," Beatrix barked at him.

He did as he was told.

"Bryan!" wailed Sascha Duffy.

142

"If you've hurt her . . ." he began, before realising how stupid that was.

Beatrix didn't respond.

"Come on, Rose. Please. This isn't necessary."

Faulkner came up behind him and fastened cable ties around both wrists.

"Get in the car," Beatrix said.

Faulkner yanked him backwards to the Freelander. Duffy kept his eyes on Beatrix as he stumbled. But he didn't resist.

Faulkner had found an empty building on the outskirts of the city. It had been bombed during the war and repairs, if they had started at all, had been sporadic. The building looked as if it had been used as a foundry at some point in its history, but it had been wrecked. The windows had all been blown in, and one of the walls had partially collapsed.

They saw no one as they drew up. There was an underground car park, and Faulkner drove inside. Beatrix followed in the Audi.

The car park was empty, save for four cars that had been damaged when the factory was bombed and then scavenged in the aftermath. Faulkner pulled up next to them, adjacent to the open doorway with stairs leading up.

They followed them up to the ground floor. It was in a terrible mess. It was a wide open space with large pieces of industrial machinery. There was a large furnace, moulding machines, grinders, ladles and saws. The floor was littered with fragments of glass, and as they crunched across it, a flock of birds exploded up from a roost beneath an overturned shot-blast machine. The floor was slicked with their guano, and rainwater that had fallen through the holes in the roof had gathered in stagnant puddles.

"Nice place," Duffy said.

Faulkner led the way to another room at the rear of the space. It was furnished with plastic chairs and tables. There was a metal counter, refrigerators and a large range. It must have been the factory canteen.

"There's a walk-in fridge over there," Faulkner said, pointing at the back of the room. "There's a lock on the door. Should be secure enough."

"This is perfect," she said. She turned to Duffy and his wife. "Sit," she said, indicating two of the chairs.

They did as they were told.

Faulkner covered Duffy with his pistol as Beatrix approached him.

"Listen very carefully. I'm not going to promise that you can get out of this, because you know you can't, but if you do what I tell you to do, I promise I'll do you quickly and I won't touch your wife. Under the circumstances, after what you did to me, that's a pretty good deal."

"What do you want?"

"Your company has two people in custody. You're going to help us to release them."

"Who?"

"The first one is Mackenzie West."

Duffy laughed bitterly. "You know I can't do that."

Beatrix stared at him, hard. "You just need to tell me where he is."

"And if I don't?"

"You don't need to ask me that."

He flinched, anger and frustration on his face. He knew he was finished. He nodded at Faulkner and tried to change the subject. "He's with the Group?"

"Yes."

"So he's here for West, then? That's the mission?"

"Never mind that," Faulkner said.

"I know—you can't say. It doesn't matter. I know that's why you're here. MI6 wants to stir things up so that the Iraqis cancel the lease and give it to BP. We knew that was coming."

"Are you going to help us?" Faulkner said.

He looked at him with a derisive sneer. "What are you? Number Ten? Number Eleven?"

Faulkner said nothing.

"You're Twelve, aren't you?"

He scowled at him.

"Jesus. They sent you a baby," Duffy said, grinning at Beatrix. "What are you, his wet nurse?"

Faulkner glowered.

"Who's the new commanding officer?" Duffy asked.

Faulkner gritted his teeth.

Duffy turned back to Beatrix. "It's Michael Pope, isn't it? I know he didn't have all that much to choose from after what you and Milton did to that team in Russia, but, my God, *seriously?*"

"You know about Russia?" she said.

"We know all about that."

Beatrix seized on that. "Control told you?"

He looked her with a sudden glint of cunning. "You know that I know where he is, don't you? I know he's the one you really want. He's responsible for what happened to you. What would you say if I gave him up? I could tell you where he is and how you could get to him. Would that be enough for you and me to call it quits?"

"For you and me to be quits, I'd have to shoot your lovely wife in the head and then I'd shoot you. So no, that wouldn't make us quits. It wouldn't even be close."

"Come on!"

"Where's West?"

"Go to Hell."

"Last chance, Duffy. Where is he?"

"Fuck you." He spat at her and then craned his head so that he could look back at Faulkner. "And fuck you, too."

"Okay."

Beatrix stepped back. Sascha Duffy's chair was behind an overturned table. Beatrix reached down to pick up the table and pushed it so that the edge bumped up against the woman's chest. She took out one of her throwing knives and, going around behind her, she sliced through the cable tie. She reached out, fastened her fingers around Sascha's right wrist and pressed her hand down against the table. Duffy started to protest, but she raised her left hand to forestall him.

She was reluctant to involve the woman. She had no wish to hurt her. After all, she had done nothing to her. Beatrix was quite certain that she had never even heard her name before. Her involvement was just bad luck. It was unfortunate that she was married to Duffy. It was unfortunate that she was here, with him, in Basra. It was unfortunate that she could be used as a lever against him.

She thought of Mysha. She had made a promise to her, and she meant to keep it.

Sascha Duffy was a means to an end.

There were other ways that she could get the information that she needed, but they would be messy and unpleasant. Time was pressing, and this, she knew, would be the quickest way.

"Spread your fingers, please," she said.

"What?"

"Spread your fingers."

"No."

"It'll be much better if you do."

She raised the knife, tip pointing down at the back of the woman's hand.

"Sascha!"

The woman spread her fingers just as Beatrix stabbed down at the table, the blade tapping into the wood between her thumb and index finger. Beatrix raised it and brought it down again, the blade pecking between Sascha's index finger and forefinger, then again between her forefinger and ring finger, then again between her ring finger and little finger.

Beatrix started again, a little more quickly.

"I used to be good at this," she said as she moved the blade with fluid speed. "I could do it faster, but that was a long time ago. I'm older now. The reflexes . . . well," she darted the knife faster and faster, "I'm getting up to how fast I'd be comfortable doing this if it was my hand and not your wife's."

The colour had drained from Sascha Duffy's face, and she couldn't speak.

"A little bit faster, then?"

"No," Duffy protested. "Stop. *Stop!*"

Beatrix raised her fist to the height of her head and then slammed the blade down, hard, the point buried into the wood between the woman's thumb and forefinger, millimetres from the fleshy web that joined them.

"Stop, Rose. Stop. That's enough."

"Shall we try again?"

"I'll tell you what you want."

"Where's West?"

"A safe house."

"Where?"

"We have an office."

"You were there yesterday?"

"You were following me?"

"That was the office?"

He jerked his head in a nod. "Yes."

"How safe?"

"It won't be easy to get him out."

"We'll worry about that later."

"Guarded?" Faulkner asked.

"Of *course* it's guarded," he said derisively.

"That's better, Duffy," Beatrix said. "Now, the second man. His name is Faik al-Kaysi. Your men shot and killed his mother and arrested him."

"Name's not familiar."

"But?"

"But we've scooped up plenty of troublemakers recently. It's possible. What's he got to do with you?"

She ignored his question. "Where would he be?"

"I don't know. I'll have to make a call."

Beatrix frowned at that.

"I can't tell you what I don't know, Rose. We give them all to the Iraqis. Local police. God knows what they do with them afterwards. He's probably in al-Mina."

"Local prison?"

"Yes."

Beatrix turned to Faulkner. "Give me your phone."

"I don't know, Rose . . . You think that's a good idea?"

"Give it to me." She pulled out the P226 and pressed it against Sascha Duffy's right temple. "It's fine. If he says anything I don't like, I'll shoot her and then I'll shoot him. And he knows I'd do it, too. Don't you, Duffy?"

"Don't worry. I'm not going to do anything stupid."

Duffy spoke on the phone for five minutes. He asked for details on Faik al-Kaysi and then he waited as whoever it was on the other end looked into it. Beatrix watched him carefully, the Sig pressed against Sascha Duffy's head the entire time. The woman was stock still, hardly breathing, bloodless. She heard the muffled voice of the other person as information was relayed and watched as Duffy's eyebrows rose.

He ended the call and handed the phone back to her. There was a bitter little smirk on his lips.

"Don't think there's much you can do about this one."

"What do you mean?"

"We did arrest him, after the thing at the oilfield. He's in al-Mina, like I thought, but he's been convicted of murder. There was a riot the day before yesterday. Several of the guards were killed. They're going to hang him and some of the others."

"Where?"

"In the prison yard."

"When?"

"After prayers. Tomorrow morning. First light."

Beatrix gave a crisp nod. "Thank you."

"What now?"

"Get in there," she said, pointing to the walk-in fridge.

"Come on, Rose, I'm helping you out. This isn't necessary."

"You know it is, Duffy. Don't waste my time. Get in the back or I'll shoot you now."

"Alright, alright," he said. "Fine."

Faulkner followed the two of them back to the fridge, and once they were inside, he locked the door and then slid an iron bar through the two door handles.

"You can't be serious?" Faulkner said in an urgent hiss as soon as he was done.

"About what?"

"Getting this Iraqi boy?"

"Deadly serious."

"There's two of us. *Two.* You want to plan a jail break? How are we going to do that?"

"There's always a way. These will be untrained, badly armed guards. And they have no idea we're coming. There's no better tactical advantage than surprise."

"We don't have the kit."

"No," she accepted, "that I do agree with. You're going to need to set up another meeting with the quartermaster. As soon as you can. He needs to come here."

"What about these two?"

"You think anyone will hear them out here if they start making a noise?"

"Probably not. I didn't see anyone around yesterday."

"Good."

"What else?"

"We stay here tonight. I'll scout the prison tomorrow, and then we can sort out the gear we'll need."

"Anything else?"

"I'm going to need to speak to Michael Pope."

Chapter Twenty-Six

They slept at the foundry that night. Beatrix awoke early and took Sascha Duffy's Audi and drove north, where Basra ran up against the Shatt Al-Aarab watercourse. She drove by the al-Mina football club, where twenty or thirty young-sters were kicking a ball across the parched yellow grass, and then by the Al-Tahreer General Hospital. She passed buildings that had been wrecked in the war and had still not been repaired, pylons that had been torn down, their cables stolen. On the horizon, gas flares leeched dirty smears of grey smoke into the sky.

It was eight in the morning and it was already hot, dizzy-ingly hot, and there was only so much that the air-conditioning in the car could do. Beatrix was sweating by the time she reached the al-Mina prison. It had been built by the Americans after the capacity in the nearby al-Ma'aqal had been exceeded. It was small by Western standards, with just four hundred inmates, and it was already overcrowded. It didn't look particularly substantial. Beatrix thought of the great Victorian edifices in London and Manchester, their vaulting brick walls and their sense of impregnability, and this collection of prefabricated buildings seemed wispy by comparison. The facility was encircled by razor-topped fences, twelve feet high, and those were protected by concrete baulks. The main entrance was a slab of concrete with a gate cut in the middle. The buildings beyond looked like warehouses. An Iraqi flag flew from a building that Beatrix guessed was used for administration.

She knew all about the reputations of Iraqi jails. Saddam had used them as depositories for anyone who had the nerve to challenge the regime, and once you were inside, there was no coming out. There were stories of what had happened in Basra's prisons during the time the British were here, too.

She was a hundred feet away from the gates. She didn't want to get any closer.

She looked around. The surrounding area had a collection of buildings that had been damaged during the war. Repairs had started on some of them but had since been paused. The insurgency had forced foreign contractors away, and they had still to return.

That suited Beatrix very well.

She was able to approach a nearby three-storey building without arousing suspicion. A metal door, chained and bolted, prevented access to the front, but the ground-floor windows were protected only by plasterboard, and Beatrix was able to force her way inside. It looked as if the place was being refitted as an office. The exterior cladding was missing in places, and the interior consisted of barren concrete surfaces and open apertures where doors and windows would eventually be fitted. Beatrix found the central stairwell and climbed to the second floor.

She made her way across the dusty, unfinished floor to the side of the building that overlooked the prison. The windows this high were open and unguarded, and she edged ahead while crouched low until she was confident that she wouldn't be observed from the street below.

She stood to the side of the window, took out her binoculars and quickly scouted the prison.

There were guards on foot in front of the main entrance and another two in a thirty-foot-high watchtower that looked over it. She focussed on them: they were toting rifles, probably Tabuks, the modified version of the Zastava M70 that the Iraqi army used. They were reliable weapons, chambered for 7.62x39mm rounds, meaning the rifle had a maximum effective range of six hundred metres. Even then, it was hopeless unless you were no more than two hundred metres away from the target. It was only good for "spray and pray," and Beatrix was not concerned about the threat that it posed. In any event, they would neutralise them first of all.

She examined the walls and the buildings. They looked as flimsy from up here as they had from the street.

An idea began to form.

She noticed a structure was being erected in the courtyard between two of the larger buildings. A wooden floor on stilts had been constructed with a staircase to one side. A long frame was lying in the dust, consisting of two 3-metre-long posts that had been fashioned into square diameters with a third post, perhaps two metres long, fixed between them and supported by braces. There were slots in the wooden floor where the frame might be inserted. A man was working on the frame, using a power saw to cut out a notch in the middle of the shorter post.

It was a gallows.

The notch would be where the noose would be fitted.

It was mid-afternoon when she returned to the derelict foundry. There was a rental car outside the building. Beatrix was expecting company, but experience had taught her that assumptions were dangerous. She took the Sig and shoved it into the waistband of her trousers.

Faulkner was in the canteen with the Group Fifteen quartermaster.

"Hello again," he said. "You wanted some extra hardware?"

"Something came up. Different needs."

He indicated Faulkner. "So he said."

"Can you help?"

He nodded. "I can. I have just what you need."

Beatrix had called Faulkner with the list of equipment that they required. The man took a long canvas bag from the floor and placed it on one of the canteen tables. He unzipped the bag and took out an M40 bolt action sniper rifle. "Not easy to get this on short notice," he said. "A friend of a friend had it. It was left behind after Enduring Freedom. It's not the best example I've ever seen, but it'll do. It should be good enough for what you want."

Beatrix took the parts, examined them and then assembled them with expert hands. The M40 was standard issue for the United States Marine Corps. Bolt action, a five-round integral box magazine, chambered for 7.62x51mm NATO rounds, accurate to up to nine hundred metres. It needed a good cleaning and a splash of oil, but it would serve their purposes.

"Ammunition?"

The quartermaster reached into the bag and took out a box of rounds.

"Sight?"

He took out a Schmidt and Bender Police Marksman II 3-12x50 dayscope. This, at least, looked brand new. He went back to the bag and collected a swivel-type bi-pod.

"Good," she said.

Finally, he took a pair of walkie-talkies. "Best I could do, I'm afraid."

Beatrix took them. They looked like they were twenty years old. As long as they worked, they would suffice. She tossed one across the room to Faulkner.

"Do you need anything else?" the quartermaster asked.

"No," she said. "This will be fine."

"Very good."

He nodded with satisfaction and left them.

"Well?" Faulkner said.

She took out the map that she had drawn this morning and spread it on the table. "There are buildings all around the prison. Most of them are empty. Construction sites. No guards. Easy to slip in and out. You won't have any problems. This one here"—she stabbed a finger against the paper—"this is the one. Perfect view into the yard. Are you happy with the rifle?"

Faulkner hefted it. "Looks fine. Range?"

"Three hundred yards."

"Then there won't be a problem. You don't need to worry about me holding up my end."

"I'm not worried," she said. "You'll do fine."

Faulkner's cellphone was on the table. It started to vibrate.

Faulkner picked it up. "Hello, sir," he said. "Yes. She's here. Hold on." He offered the phone to Beatrix. "It's Pope."

She looked at it dubiously.

"It's safe. Encrypted."

She put the phone to her ear. "Hello, Pope."

"What are you doing, Beatrix?"

"Stop worrying."

"Stop? Faulkner tells me . . ."

"I'll do what I promised."

"But?"

"But I need to do something else first."

155

"But you're still—"

"Yes," she cut him off. "I'm still going to get West for you."

"What about Duffy?"

"We've got him with us. He's being very helpful."

"In exchange for what?" He sounded dubious.

"We have his wife, too."

"Okay . . ." He sounded reluctant, but there was nothing that he could do. He needed Beatrix. She knew that perfectly well. They both knew that Faulkner was too green to extract Mackenzie West alone. "What do you need?"

"I met a girl. An Iraqi girl. She helped me out, and so I'm going to return the favour."

"Philanthropy, Beatrix? That's not like you."

I want to do something right.

And this is right.

"Rose?"

"She's twelve years old. Her mother was killed by Duffy's men. Her brother was detained and passed to the police. They're going to execute him in six hours. They've already built the gallows. She doesn't have anyone else, Pope. It's me or nothing."

"We don't have any influence in Basra anymore, Beatrix. I'm not going to be able to put any pressure on, especially not in six hours."

"I don't need you to put pressure on. Even if you could, there wouldn't be time."

"So?"

"Just listen. I'm going to go in and get him out."

"What?"

"*Listen.* I've scouted it. The security is weak. It's easily breached. Getting him out isn't the problem; it's what happens next. He won't be able to stay in Basra. They know where he lives. They'll just come and get him again. I need you to arrange for him and his sister to get out of Iraq. They have family in Kuwait. You need to get them over the border."

There was a pause.

"Pope?"

"Yes," he said. "That might be possible. We have assets in theatre. I can get them to the border."

"Fine. Good. Get it sorted. Do it now. Just tell Faulkner where you need us to bring them. We'll do the rest."

Chapter Twenty-Seven

"Wake up."

Faik was not asleep.

There was a window in the cell they used for condemned men. It was small, barred and set high in the wall, but he was able to look out into a small parcel of sky. The city was enduring one of its daily brownouts, and most of the lights in the prison were out. As a result, it looked especially dark. There were clouds, too, oil-coloured clouds that rolled over the lightening sky like a slick. A storm was coming.

Faik opened his eyes. There was a sudden, discordant clatter as the guard dragged a metal mug back and forth across the bars of the cell. The nine other prisoners made no noise. There was no muttering and grumbling. Faik doubted whether any of them had slept, either. The truth of the day that they had dreaded was impressed onto them indelibly. They could not forget it, not even for a moment.

He had been moved from isolation last night. There were ten men in this cell. Faik was lying tight between two of them. There was only just enough space for them all to lie down together, and not enough for it to be possible to negotiate a path to the open cesspit without treading on hands and feet and waking the others. It was irrelevant, really. He opened his eyes now to aches in his body from tiredness and from lying on the bare concrete floor, and his thoughts were sluggish.

"Wake up, you dogs. A big day for you all today."

Faik closed his eyes again. Perhaps he could wish it away.

"Get back from the door," one of the guards ordered.

The metal scraped against the stone as the door was pushed back. The prisoners pressed themselves away from it and from the guards who now stepped inside.

"Three of you today," one of them said. It was Donkey. He paused and turned to exchange a sneering grin with one of his colleagues.

He was carrying a cattle prod. He stabbed out with it three times.

"You, you and you."

Faik was the third.

He struggled to his haunches and then tried to back away.

But there was nowhere to go.

His knees started to shake uncontrollably.

The guards rushed into the small cell. They took the first man by the arms and hauled him outside. The man was cuffed and shackled. He was too stunned to struggle.

The second man, an oil worker who had been arrested at the same time as Faik, was ready for them. He swung a punch at the first man, the blow sinking into the man's gut, and then he threw himself at the other two. There was a crackle of electricity as the cattle prod was rammed into his chest. The voltage dropped him to the floor of the cell just as quickly as if he had been drilled in the head. He was still twitching as the guards pulled him outside and cuffed him.

They came back for Faik. He tried to resist, but he was smaller than they were, and he hadn't slept or eaten properly for days. He was as weak as a kitten. They tugged him outside and cuffed him. A sack was pulled over his head, and he was manhandled down the corridor. They turned once, twice, and then a door was opened, and fresh morning air kissed his sweating skin.

"Please," he said. "Please, don't. I have a sister. Our parents are dead. She needs me."

"You should have thought of that," Donkey hissed into his ear.

The arms on either side of him were withdrawn, and unsupported, he fell to his knees.

The sack was removed.

He was in the main yard, the walls topped with coiled razor wire a short distance away from him. There was a crowd of people inside the yard. Several hundred. Prisoners, roused from their sleep to partake in a chastening spectacle. Guards, too. Some of them had cameras. The atmosphere was a strange mixture of the festive and the frightened. The prisoners knew that the condemned men could just as easily be them. The guards knew that, too. It was a chance to bolster their position. They would use the morning's display to reinforce their authority.

Fear made men docile.

Faik stared. In front of the three of them, just a few paces away, was a wooden construction that had not been in place the last time that he had been given his hour of exercise in the yard. It was a raised wooden platform with a thick vertical pillar and a horizontal post forming a cross-braced T. A noose dangled from the post, turning gently in the breeze. There was a trapdoor beneath the noose.

As Faik watched, the trapdoor was tested: it suddenly gaped open, slamming up against the underside of the platform, revealing a long drop to the ground below.

The sky overhead was as black as pitch. There was a flicker of light in the distance and then, a second later, a monstrous blare of thunder.

Donkey took him under the arm.

"You first."

"Please!"

The guard dragged Faik upright and heaved him over to the steps that led up to the gallows.

Chapter Twenty-Eight

They slept in the canteen. Beatrix managed only a few hours, and those were fitful, assailed by her worries and fears: Isabella, the task she had set for herself and the need to complete it before her time ran out. When she eventually abandoned the pretence of rest, it was three in the morning. Her body spasmed with pain; it felt like she had an inch of water in her lungs, and she ached with the fatigue. She took a Zomorph, and then when that only dulled the edges of the pain, she took another. She dared not take more.

It all started now.

None of what she was planning was going to be easy, and she needed to be on her game.

Faulkner awoke a little after her. He found her outside, staring into the darkness.

"Still want to do this?" he said.

She nodded. "You know what you're doing?"

"Yes."

"As soon as I get him, you need to get down and get the car started. We'll have a minute or two when they're working out what's hit them. It won't last, though. As soon as someone gets them organised, we'll be outgunned. We won't want to be anywhere near there then."

"I've got it."

"Good."

"Synchronise watches." She pulled back her sleeve. "I've got four-fifteen."

Faulkner adjusted his watch accordingly. "Four-fifteen, check."

"I'll see you in an hour and three-quarters."

Beatrix sat in the driver's seat of the Audi. She was parked five hundred feet away from the entrance to the prison. She dared not wait any closer than that. She watched through her binoculars as activity increased in the yard. Everything was as she remembered it from yesterday: the high fence, the gimcrack walls.

She narrowed her focus. The office block was between her and the prison. The Freelander should have been parked in a side street, out of direct sight of the prison but close enough to be started quickly when they needed it.

She had clipped the walkie-talkie onto her jacket. She thumbed the channel.

"One, Twelve. Comms check."

There was a crackle of static, and for a moment she doubted that they were going to work.

"Twelve, One," Faulkner said. "Copy that. I can hear you."

"What can you see?"

"They're getting ready. The gallows are up. There's a small crowd. At least three hundred. Maybe four."

"The guards?"

"Two in the watchtower with rifles. I can see fifteen in the yard. Eight of them are armed. Automatics and semi-automatics."

"Anything else I need to know?"

"No. You still sure about this?"

"Just tell me when they bring them out."

Beatrix had the bullpup F2000 Tactical TR on the seat next to her. She rested her hands on the steering wheel and slowly squeezed it tighter and tighter. This was the worst kind of jerry-rigged plan, thrown together too quickly with too little research. She would never have agreed to it if it had been presented to her. There were so many things that could go wrong.

The sun was rising into the sky, but it was invisible behind the thick blanket of black clouds.

"Twelve, One," the walkie-talkie crackled. "Here we go. They're bringing them out."

She reached down and started the engine. "You ready?"

"On your mark."

"You better be able to shoot straight, Faulkner. I'm going to need you." She fed the engine revs and let off the handbrake. The car started towards the prison gates. "Here we go."

Faulkner was pleased.

Beatrix knew what she was doing.

The unfinished office was an excellent overlook position. He would have liked to run a laser range to gauge things properly, but they hadn't been able to get the equipment for that, and besides, he was already pretty close to the targets. He worked out a crude firing solution on the watchtower and then on the yard beyond it, and noted the details in the logbook by his side. Satisfied, he glassed the entire area, fixing the landmarks in his mind's eye.

The rain had started to fall, and it had quickly fallen faster and faster until it was a deluge, sheeting down, a virtual torrent that made sighting much more difficult than it would have been if they had been conducting this operation yesterday.

But that was an excuse, and Faulkner dismissed it. He didn't need excuses.

The prisoners were arranged in front of the gallows, with armed guards to the rear. They were dressed in orange prison-issue jumpsuits and had been dragged out into the rain to watch three of their number shuffled off this mortal coil. It had been planned as an instructive lesson for them. A reminder of what happened when you went up against the will of the government.

He watched the sentries in the watchtower for a moment. Two of them, both with Zastava M70 rifles, a little miserable from the rain by the looks of things, their attention distracted by the people in the yard behind their tower.

He laid the crosshairs of the rifle on one of the sentries.

His finger rested on the trigger housing.

He gauged the distance again.

Smoke was drifting out of a chimney in the prison's roof. He used it to judge the wind: two minutes left.

He held the target in the sights, aiming for the centre mass.

He heard Beatrix's voice over the radio.

"One, Twelve. Fire when ready."

He waited for another deep roll of thunder, louder than his rifle. It came, rolling over the rooftops, and Faulkner exhaled and gently pulled straight back on the trigger. The rifle fired, the 7.62mm bullet punching into the sentry just right of centre. He staggered back and slumped down in the corner of the enclosed platform. The second sentry gawked at his fallen colleague, realising, too late, that he would have been better served dropping to the floor himself. Faulkner turned the rifle on him, jacked in a new round, and hammered the guard with a second chest shot.

"Twelve, One. Two hits. Both sentries down."

"Anyone notice?"

"Negative."

"I'm going in. Give them something to think about when I get close."

Faulkner fed a fresh round into his rifle and looked for a new target. He found one, a guard near the gallows, and held him nice and steady in the middle of the sight.

He heard the engine of the Audi as Beatrix roared down the road.

There was no need to mask this shot.

He wanted them to know.

He exhaled a half breath and pulled the trigger.

Slow and smooth.

Straight and steady.

Squeeze.

The rifle bucked against his shoulder, and the boom rang around the neighbourhood. In the scope, Faulkner watched the bullet slam into the chest of the target. He dropped to his knees and then fell to one side, his organs pulped where the bullet had exploded inside him. Faulkner used his thumb and two fingers to jack a fresh round into the chamber and swept the scope around the yard.

Chaos.

The Audi rushed at the gates, gathering pace, the engine screaming.

He fed another round into the rifle and sighted again.

The car smashed through the gate.

Beatrix pulled down on the handle and kicked the door open. There was pandemonium outside. One of the guards brought up his rifle and aimed it at her. The rifle cracked, but the shot went wide, missing by a fraction and thudding into one of the watchtower's wooden struts.

Faulkner's rifle boomed out again, and the shooter's head splattered in a pink mist.

Another rifle fired, the shot caroming into the car's windscreen. It shattered in a bright cascade of glass.

Two guards appeared in the doorway of the main building. Beatrix hit the ground and rolled, bringing up the F2000 and squeezing off two 3-round bursts. The guards tottered as they were drilled, both stumbling back into the building.

She assessed. The yard was full of yellow dust that had been thrown up by her entrance, and there was a clamour of alarms, confused shouts from the prisoners and the panic of the guards. She focussed on the three men in orange prison jumpsuits who were restrained with shackles around their wrists and ankles.

She had anticipated that.

The walkie-talkie crackled. "Two police cars incoming," Faulkner said. "Half a mile away, coming in fast. You need to be quick."

"I've got it," she said as she hurried around to the trunk of the Audi.

She took a pair of long-handled bolt cutters from the trunk and ran to the prisoners.

"I'm here to help you," she called out in Arabic.

She had memorised Faik's face, and she found him quickly. He was dazed and fearful, and he shied away as she reached out and took him by the elbow.

"What do you want?"

"I'm getting you out."

She could see that she was confusing him: her perfect Arabic, her blonde hair, the fact that she was so obviously a Westerner. His hands were shaking as she slid the teeth of the cutters around the chain that connected the shackles at the ankles and, grunting with effort, closed the handles and sheared through it.

"Help us too!" said one of the others.

"They are killing us!"

Beatrix knew that she didn't have time, but she couldn't leave them. The Iraqis would shoot them as soon as they had reinforcements in place. She took the cutters and cleaved through their ankle shackles. It took fifteen seconds that she didn't have, and when she was done, she was sweating from the effort, and the sirens from the police cars were almost upon them.

One of the guards had crawled behind a collection of oil drums. Beatrix hadn't seen him. He crouched and took aim with his rifle.

She caught him in the corner of her eye.

Damn it.

The M40 boomed again and the guard was drilled in the chest. He crumpled out of sight.

"Thank you," Beatrix said.

Faulkner's voice crackled back to her. "You need to get out of there."

She had taken her eye off the prisoners for a moment. They scattered. Some of them ran towards the gate, and before Beatrix could do anything to intervene, a guard who had been waiting just outside it swung out of cover and sprayed them with automatic gunfire. One of the prisoners was cut down, crumpling into the dust of the yard.

Beatrix aimed the bullpup and fired.

Her rounds went wide, peppering the concrete post and forcing the guard back into cover.

"Faulkner . . ."

The rifle boomed.

"Got him."

Faik watched in abject terror. He ran away from her and the gate, instinctively sprinting for cover in the only place he knew he would find it.

He ran back inside the prison.

"Faik!"

Two police cars skidded to a stop outside the gate.

"They're here."

"He's gone inside," she called back.

"Rose . . ."

"I've got to go and get him."

"It's too late. Get out."

"I'm going after him."

The prison was a hellhole. It was badly constructed, and even though it was new, corners had been cut and it was already falling to pieces. There was a reception area and then a series of corridors that led away like the threads of a spider's web. One of the gates was standing open, and she saw the flash of Faik's orange jumpsuit as he rushed through it.

"Faik!" she called. "Stop!"

He didn't stop.

Not good.

"I'm here to help you."

She heard his bare feet slapping away on the concrete floor.

Not good at all.

She cradled the F2000 and sprinted after him. There were no windows, and the light soon faded away, leaving her to make her way through a crepuscular gloom that was ameliorated only by a handful of overhead striplights, many of them flickering unhealthily. The occasional overhead light well admitted slanting shafts of daylight that served no useful purpose, save, perhaps, as cruel reminders of the world outside.

Faik hadn't gotten very far. She found him cowering against the wall in a long corridor that ended with a locked metal gate. The corridor beyond the gate had cells on both sides.

She let the F2000 hang on its sling and approached him cautiously. His hair was matted, clotted with dried blood, and his face bore the unmistakeable signs of a heavy beating. There was a bruise across his cheekbone that was striated with the markings from the sole of a boot.

He spoke in Arabic. "Leave me alone."

"I'm here to get you out."

"Leave me!"

"You're Faik al-Kaysi?"

He shrunk away.

"I met your sister. She told me what had happened to you."

"But what . . ." He was pitifully confused. "Who are you?"

"I'm a friend. And we need to get out of here."

"Why do you do this? What do you want from me?"

"Just to take you home. Mysha would like to see you again."

The mention of her name seemed to penetrate the fear clouding his mind. "Mysha?"

"Yes," she said. She held out a hand. Every second made it less likely they would be able to leave in one piece. She had to fight the temptation to yank him upright.

He took her hand and got to his feet.

"Stay behind me," she commanded.

This might get a little hot.

Michael Pope moved to the edge of the building and took a quick glimpse down onto the prison yard fifty yards below. He had watched as Rose and Faulkner had commenced their operation. It was an unsophisticated plan, reliant on the fear that would be wrought by an accurate sniper against a crowd of easy targets and then the shock of a frontal assault. A blunt cudgel of a plan, but as Faulkner had explained to him last night, there was no time to arrange anything more subtle.

It might have worked, too, for all its flaws.

Faulkner had taken a well-scouted firing position, and for a soldier with aim as good as his, hitting the guards from that kind of range was like shooting fish in a barrel. Pope had counted eight accurate shots before Faulkner's position had been exposed.

Beatrix had cut through the confused guards with ease. She would have been able to escape again, too, if the prisoner she was so determined to release had not turned tail and disappeared back into the building again.

Now, though, Beatrix was in a very dangerous position.

Faulkner had abandoned his eyrie and was no longer able to provide covering fire. The surviving guards were beginning to pull themselves together. And the police reinforcements were well organised. They had sealed the breached entrance with two cars and then had fallen back into cover where they could safely concentrate their fire.

Pope heard the rumble of the big engine through the radio and then from the street below. He looked back over the edge of the roof at the big Manage Risk APC and watched grimly as it rolled up to the two police cars. It had its forward searchlights lit, powerful beams that traced blinding streaks through the gloom.

Shit.

Rose was trapped inside a prison.

A dangerous position? No, he corrected himself. It wasn't dangerous.

It was hopeless.

Or it *would* have been hopeless.

Pope had followed Beatrix to Iraq. It was in direct contravention of Stone's explicit orders, but he wanted to be on the ground. He had been a soldier for all of his adult life, and he had always known that he would find the transition to riding a desk difficult.

It had been impossible in this instance.

Rose was a brilliant operative, even now, even after all this time, but she was impulsive. She was bordering on rash. He had guessed, correctly as it turned out, that she was liable to go off the reservation, and when that happened, he wanted the added flexibility that being on the ground would afford him.

He needed Mackenzie West taken out of the country in one piece. He had only just assumed his new role. This should have been an easy enough job, even given the fact that he had been asked to use an agent who was no longer on the books of the Group. Go in, get the target, exfiltrate him. The business with Duffy should have been simple enough, too. Duffy must have guessed that he was on Rose's shit list, but he wouldn't have expected her to find him so quickly after she had taken out Joshua Joyce.

But Rose had complicated things. He didn't know her well, but he knew her well enough to know that there would have been no point in trying to change her mind about this excursion. Faulkner could have tried, but he wouldn't have gotten anywhere. Pope could have tried, too, but he would have had no greater success, and he would have had to reveal his presence to speak to her properly. There was no point.

No.

This farrago was a complication, but it shouldn't have been insurmountable.

172

But now this.

He glanced down at the Grizzly and the blocked gateway and the confidence that was flooding back into the routed guards.

This.

He couldn't have a failure on his résumé.

And he wanted to help Rose, too.

He had meant everything that he had said to Stone.

It was the least that he could do.

———

Beatrix pushed Faik behind her and held him back with one arm. She had fallen back to just inside the entrance to the main building. The lobby was behind them, the Plexiglas-fronted counter that visitors would pass through before being admitted into the guts of the building. She didn't want to go deeper inside again. It would have been safer, for a short while, but they would have been trapped. There would be nowhere to go once they were back there again, and it would just be a matter of time before they were hunted down and shot.

Their chances in the other direction were better, but not by very much.

The guards were still in disarray, but that wouldn't last.

"One, Twelve. Report."

"I'm in the car."

"Can you see anything?"

"Trouble. An APC just went by. Heading to the front gate."

Wonderful.

"Can you get to me?"

"Not easily. They've blocked the gates."

She gripped the rifle tightly.

Faik took her shoulder. "What is happening?"

"Stay there," she said.

"Why are we waiting here?"

"Stay back," she said sharply. "Wait. If you don't, you'll get shot. Understand?"

"Yes," he said timidly.

She lowered the rifle and, crouching low, slid around the corner of the building.

She saw the Grizzly just as the 12.7mm machine gun started to fire. The big rounds pulverised the building, a cloud of concrete chips exploded into the air and blooms of dust were thrown out with every fresh impact. The noise was tremendous: the thunderous clatter of the machine gun and the heavy thumps as the rounds slammed into the brick and stone.

Beatrix dropped to her belly and scrabbled back behind the corner.

This was very bad.

"Twelve, One. Come in."

"Copy. What?"

"Hold position, One."

"For what?"

"You're about to get a chance to make a move. Be ready. Twelve out."

Pope reached back to the large canvas bag that he had brought onto the roof with him. He dragged it closer, and working quickly, he unzipped it. He thumbed the radio.

"Pope, Twelve."

"Copy that, Pope. What do you want me to do?"

"Sitrep?"

"I'm still here. Heavy activity. Another APC has just gone by."

"I hear it. Are you still hidden?"

"Affirmative."

"And ready to go?"

"Affirmative."

"On my mark."

Pope reached into the bag and took out an RPG-2. It was an anti-tank grenade launcher, a long tube open at both ends. It was a little higher than his waist when he laid it out on the roof next to him. The launcher was Russian and old. There were hundreds of them swilling around the black economy, and it had been easy for the quartermaster to source. It was much less sophisticated than the LAWs that Pope had been trained to use in the Regiment, but he was close to his target, and all he had to do was aim and fire. It would suit his purposes well enough.

He raised himself to his haunches, hefted the launcher onto his shoulder and held on to both grips. Taking a breath to steady his nerves, he stood up and stepped to the edge of the roof and looked down onto the street below.

The Grizzly was firing into the prison yard, concentrating its destructive attention on a corner of the main building. The wall had been chewed all the way back to its steel columns, a ragged tear as if something monstrous had taken a bite out of it.

He sighted the APC.

"Pope, Twelve. Ready?"

"Twelve, Pope. Copy that."

"Now!"

He pulled the trigger.

———

Beatrix knew the sound that an RPG's propellant made as it ignited: the quick, sibilant whoosh. She pressed herself back against the wall, knowing that it would offer scant protection, and readied herself to die.

The impact didn't come, at least not the way that she had expected.

The explosion was farther away and much, much louder.

She ducked her head around the corner. The Grizzly that had been firing on her had been popped open, the turret torn off and thrown to the side. She was just in time to see a secondary explosion as the big diesel tank detonated, a raging column of orange fire that scorched up and out of the wreckage of the hull. Debris flew hundreds of feet into the air and razored shrapnel peppered the wall with high-pitched chings.

No time for questions.

"Faik! After me—run!"

She sprinted into the yard and hoped that he was wise enough to follow her lead.

The Grizzly was spewing black smoke and steam into the morning air, the rain still slamming down. The guards, still barely recovering their composure, had either been thrown to the floor or had turned to face the sound of the explosion.

They had taken their attention away from Beatrix.

That was unfortunate for them.

She opened fire as she ran, holding the rifle with both hands and pumping bullets from the hip. She carved a path through them, the rounds either taking down their targets or forcing them into a second panicked retreat.

She heard the roar of a powerful engine from the other side of the wall and then the squeal of rubber biting on asphalt as a car skidded to a stop.

She hoped it was Faulkner.

Pope discarded the empty launcher and hurried back across the roof. There was a fire escape on the other side of the building, and he took the stairs two at a time, pausing on the landing to withdraw his pistol. He didn't need it. The guards in the yard had either been shot or were too stunned to think about what had just happened, and none of them reacted. There was an alley at the back of the building with just enough space for the Toyota Camry that he had rented from the Hertz counter at the airport in Kuwait City. He gripped onto the last rung and dropped the final ten feet to the ground, tossing the pistol onto the passenger seat as he slid into the car. He turned the ignition and drove quickly away from the prison.

_____

Faulkner left rubber as he gunned the engine. The police turned in the direction of the SUV at the sound of the engine. One of them raised a rifle. There was no chance for him to fire it. He heard the crackle of automatic gunfire and saw the muzzle flash as Beatrix emerged from the building. The prisoner quailed behind her. She had a spare magazine in her left hand, pressed up against the forestock, and, as the first ran dry, she ejected it and slapped in the replacement almost without pause.

Three of the police went down, and the others scattered. Faulkner hit the brakes and slid the back around, thudding into one of the survivors full-on and sending him ten feet through the air.

He reached over and opened the doors.

Beatrix and the man ran full pelt to the car.

She almost threw Faik into the rear seat, yelling "Go!" as she stood on the sill.

He stamped on the gas and the SUV sped away.

Gunfire clattered in their direction, but none of the rounds found their mark. Beatrix returned fire, and then, as they moved out of immediate range, she slid inside and slammed the door closed.

"Who was that?"

"Who was what?"

"Don't play dumb, Faulkner. Who fired the RPG?"

"Pope."

The dial topped fifty and then sixty as Faulkner aimed away from the prison. He hammered the brakes as they approached a sharp turn, the sudden deceleration throwing them all towards the front of the car and then to the side as he yanked the wheel to the right.

"He's here?"

"He thought it might be a good idea to have a little extra backup."

"You didn't think to tell me?"

"He told me not to."

"Why not?"

They reached a junction with the main highway. Faulkner bullied his way out into the flow and then slotted out into the outside lane, flooring the pedal again.

"Why not?" she repeated.

"I don't know," Faulkner said. "You'll have to ask him. He's driving West and your boy back there to Kuwait."

Chapter Twenty-Nine

Faulkner drove them out to the shantytown on the edge of the oilfields. Faik was quiet throughout, occasionally dabbing a tentative fingertip to the bruises on his face or squinting out into the sunlight as the sun dipped down over the horizon.

"Is my sister okay?" he asked, finally.

"She is."

"How do you know her?"

"She helped me out. I'm returning the favour."

"Did she tell you what happened?"

"To your mother? Yes, she did. I'm sorry."

"The men who did it. Nothing will happen to them. They will do it again, too. They are not police. They are not military. It does not matter. The law does not apply to them."

"Some laws do," she said.

Beatrix ejected the magazine from the FN F2000 and examined it. She had fifteen rounds left.

"They will come for me now," he said. "They know where I live. My sister will not be safe."

She propped the gun in the footwell and turned all the way around. "You have family in Kuwait, don't you?"

"Yes. An uncle. But it is irrelevant. How can we leave the country? We have no papers, no money, no anything. We would . . ."

"I'm going to arrange it all for you."

"Why . . . ?"

She looked squarely at him. "You need to get your sister, pack whatever you need and then go. You're right. They will come after you. They're probably working out who has gone missing now. They might even be on their way. We need to go as soon as we get Mysha."

"You will help us?"

"I'm going to get you both into Kuwait. You'll be safe there."

———

Faulkner parked the car next to the shack. Beatrix opened the door to get out. Faik did the same, still moving slowly and with an expression of wariness on his bruised face. She could guess why. He was wondering if this was another trick. Was he being teased with the prospect of his freedom, only to have it taken away at the last moment? Worse than that, was his little sister in danger now, too?

Mysha emerged and ran to her brother. She flung her arms around him, her face pressed into his chest. He returned the embrace, picking her up and squeezing her tight. When he looked over at Beatrix, there were tears streaming down his face.

She waited for a moment as they spoke.

Faulkner stood alongside her. "You cut that pretty fine," he said.

"Good shooting. It wouldn't have worked without you."

"And Pope."

"That didn't hurt," she admitted.

"What next?"

"We'll get them out of the way, and then we go and get West. Start the car. I don't want to be here any longer than we have to."

Faulkner made his way back to the Freelander. Beatrix turned back to Mysha and Faik just as the girl threw her arms around her. She untangled herself and held the girl back a little so that she could look at her.

"Thank you," Mysha said.

"You're welcome."

"You do not work in television."

"Not exactly."

"You are very kind. I don't know why you would help us like this. And I found this, too." She reached into her pocket and pulled out the roll of notes. "You must take it back. I cannot accept."

"No," Beatrix said, a little more sternly than she meant. "I have plenty of money. I want you to have it."

"I cannot . . ."

She knelt before the girl and placed both hands on her shoulders. "Mysha, please. What has happened to you and your family is not right. It makes me happy that I can help, even if it's only just a little bit. Please. You don't need to be proud. There's nothing wrong with accepting a little help now and again. And you'll need all the money you can find."

She looked across to Faik. He was watching them both, and as she caught his eye, he nodded at her.

Beatrix laid a gentle hand on the girl's cheek. "Has Faik told you what we're going to do?"

"He says we must leave."

"That's right. As soon as we can. Go and help him clean up. He's had a rough time of it. And then get the things you can't do without."

She stood and wiped a hand across her eyes.

Beatrix was thinking of Isabella as she watched the girl run back to her brother, taking his hand in hers and leading him into the house. She could not remember the last time that she had cried.

She had worried that the emotion had been smelted out of her by the cruelty of what had happened and then the long, lonely years of her exile.

But it hadn't.

She felt an ache in her heart, and she brushed away a tear. She got into the car and waited for them.

Chapter Thirty

Damon Faulkner opened the back of the Freelander. Bryan Duffy was in the compartment, hog-tied with packing tape and with a hessian sack over his head. He struggled as soon as the lid was pulled up, but it was pointless. They had secured him very carefully, and there was no way he would be able to free himself.

He tried to say something, but the rag they had taped into his mouth muffled the words.

"No point in making a fuss," Faulkner said to him. "You're not going anywhere."

There were four Mylar party balloons in the back with him. They said Happy Birthday in Arabic and were filled with helium. Faulkner snagged them quickly before they could rise out of reach.

"Back in a minute," he said, slamming the door.

He had parked fifty yards away from the Manage Risk building. There was a large stretch of scrub that filled in the void between the office block and a dried-out watercourse. A wooden pole suspended the power lines that ran to the building right across the middle of it. He forced his way through low bushes and clambered up a steep incline until he was on the scrubland, and then walked so that he was directly beneath the power line. He looked up to gauge his position, moving a little to accommodate the light, hot zephyr that was blowing in off the desert.

He spoke into the walkie-talkie. "Twelve, One," he said. "Comms check."

Beatrix Rose's voice came back: "One, Twelve. Signal's an eight."

"Also eight."

"Copy that. Status?"

"Ready when you are."

"Hold on," she said. "I'm just going in."

They had taken Duffy's keycard. Faulkner needed to wait until she had used it to get inside.

"Do it."

He released the first balloon. The wind caught it, jerking it away.

He released the second with the same result.

"One, Twelve. Status?"

"Hold on."

He waited for the breeze to fade down and released the third balloon.

It jerked left, then right, and then its ascent was halted as it bounced into the electricity wires, wedging between them.

There was a fizz and a shower of sparks as the power surged and the transformers shorted out.

"Twelve, One," he said as he walked back to the car. "Done."

"Copy that. Good work. Power's out."

"I'm going back to the car."

"Have you sorted the phone line?"

He had already fixed a wireless tap to the junction box. Any call or data that left the office would be mirrored on the laptop that was sitting in the passenger seat of the SUV. "Already done," he said.

"Good. Keep sharp. These are serious players. Eyes out, Twelve."

"Copy that. Good luck. Out."

He reached the car and opened the back again. Once more, Duffy struggled. Faulkner reached down behind his body and retrieved the FN F2000. He rested the bullpup on the chassis and took out the extra ammunition.

"I don't know exactly what you did to piss her off, but I'll tell you one thing for nothing." Duffy struggled again, harder this time. "I'm glad it's you in there and not me."

Faulkner slammed the door shut.

Beatrix was outside the entrance to the Manage Risk offices. She took the keycard she had taken from Duffy and inserted it into the reader. The lock buzzed and she pushed the door open.

"Do it."

Faulkner cut the power to the block. The lights flickered, came back on, then died. The keycard reader lost power, and when the door shut, the lock clicked as a failsafe.

Duffy had given her a walkthrough of the office layout. There were administrative offices on the first and second floors, where the business of Manage Risk in Iraq was transacted. The ground floor was a large entertainment space, with a generous reception area and three separate conference rooms. The basement, accessed from the back of the building, was where the detention suite had been built.

He'd said there would be two guards.

She anticipated more.

Beatrix clicked on her flashlight, and holding it against her extended Sig, she made her way quickly through the downstairs area. There was evidence of wealth in the beam of the torch: leather sofas, a marble reception desk, the Manage Risk logo glimmering as the light passed over it. She moved in a low crouch, and as she was opening the interconnecting door that led to the conference suite beyond, she was beset by a blast of pain that was dizzying in its intensity. She stopped, propping herself up against the desk, and waited for her head to clear. It didn't, at least not at once. A sudden surge of bile burnt up from her stomach, scorching the back of her throat as she retched onto the floor. She felt woozy, beads of sweat pricking out on her brow.

Come on.

Not now.

Come on.

Keep it together.

She wiped her mouth with the back of her hand and then reached into her pocket for the packet of Zomorph. She dry-swallowed two of the pills, took a breath and carried on.

The radio crackled with static, and then she heard Faulkner's voice again.

"Twelve, One. Copy?"

"What is it?"

"Outgoing call. Automated. There was a dead switch on the alarm. It's calling out."

"Where to?"

"I'm tracing it now. Not the police, though. I'm guessing it's an internal team."

"Eyes on it. If you see anything, I need to know. Out."

A carpeted corridor extended back from the reception, with the conference rooms on either side. The walls were glazed, and the light reflected back at her as she swung it left and right. There was no one there.

Downstairs would be different.

She found the door to the stairs and opened it as carefully as she could. The hinges were in good shape, and it was silent. Small mercies.

The stairs ended with a door. There was an emergency light at the bottom, casting an eerie green glow into the space.

She crept down the steps, her joints aching with each step.

She reached the bottom and moved to the door. It was wooden, with no window.

She could hear movement inside.

She heard a voice.

Muffled: ". . . so you tell me."

A reply: "Brownout. Wouldn't be the first."

"Like a third-world country."

"Not *like*. It *is* a third-world country."

"Thought we told them to make sure that didn't happen anymore around here."

Beatrix rested her fingertips against the door and gave it the tiniest push. It opened a fraction. It wasn't locked.

"It's Iraq, bro."

She wedged the Sig in her left armpit and took one of the M84 flash-bangs from the canteen pouch. She transferred it to her left hand.

"What the fuck you expect?"

She stood, her joints flashing with pain, and addressed the door. She pushed it open quietly, pulled the pin and rolled the grenade into the room beyond.

She turned her face away, her hand coming up in a smooth and continuous motion from the throw. She gripped the pistol, hooking her index finger through the trigger guard and sliding it so that the trigger nestled against the top joint.

The magnesium and ammonium nitrate mix detonated with an ear-splitting crack and a sunburst flash that glowed with coruscating brightness, flooding through the crack in the door.

Beatrix kicked the door all the way open and went through, shouldering it aside as it bounced back against her.

She assessed.

A medium-sized room, twenty feet by twenty feet. Two rooms off it. Substantial doors in the way. Cells, perhaps.

Two men.

They had been close to the grenade. One was on his knees, his hands pressed to his eyes. Flash blind.

The second was up against the wall, one arm braced against it while his free hand was clapped up against his left ear.

Beatrix took her finger out of the trigger guard and gripped the gun barrel tightly, using the butt to bludgeon the man nearest to her. The second man turned, reaching for a pistol on a table just out of reach, but Beatrix closed on him faster than he could move. She balanced on her left leg, lashed her right foot into his gut, and then, as he jack-knifed, she kicked straight up, the blow catching the man square on the chin. He dropped like a stone, collapsing onto the first man in an untidy mess of arms and legs.

Beatrix took the gun from the table and ejected the magazine. The first guard had a holstered pistol, and she ejected the magazine from that one, too.

"Hello? Is someone there?"

She pocketed the magazines and turned to the two doors.

"Hello?" the voice came again.

The voice was muffled, coming from behind one of the doors.

"Hello?"

She went to the door. "What's your name?" she said.

"Mackenzie West."

"Alright, Mackenzie, I'm here to get you out. I'm going to need you to stand as far away from the door as possible. I'm going to blast it open. Understand?"

"I understand."

She took the Cordtex detonation cord and a roll of sturdy double-sided tape from her pack and fixed the cord to the outline of the door, leaving a pigtail at the floor end. She primed the charge and backed out to the stairs to take cover.

"Ready?"

"I'm ready."

"Breaching in three, two, one . . ."

She fired the charge. The explosion was not large, but it was contained and amplified in the enclosed basement. There was a loud crump, a sudden discharge of dust and smoke, and then the ringing sound of the metal door as it fell to the floor.

Beatrix rounded the corner with her gun halfway up.

She recognised Mackenzie West from the picture that Pope had shown her. He was dirty, and his face, like Faik al-Kaysi's, bore the evidence of several beatings. There were bruises of different colours, some newer than the others.

He stumbled away from the wall, a fine coating of dust all over his body.

"Are you alright?"

He coughed and nodded.

"My name is Beatrix Rose. I've been sent to get you out. I know what's happened to you, why they've locked you up."

"We gotta get out. They'll kill me before they let me go."

"We are getting out. Are you fit to walk?"

"I think so."

"Stay behind me."

The radio hissed and fizzed. "Twelve, One. Copy?"

"One, Twelve. Go ahead."

"We've got trouble. A car just pulled up . . . wait, shit, there's another. Correction: *two* cars just pulled up, I'm counting four, five, six men, all armed."

"Have they seen you?"

"Negative."

"Here's what we're going to do, Twelve. Wait until they're inside. There's a reception area, self-contained. We can take them from both ends at once. On my mark, throw in a flash-bang and then pick them off. I'll do the same. Copy?"

"Twelve, One. Copy that. On your mark. Getting into position now."

Beatrix turned to West. "There's going to be some shooting. Stay behind me."

"I'm a soldier, ma'am. I understand."

She toggled radio. "One, Twelve. Update, please."

"I'm ready."

"One, Twelve. Stand by. On my mark."

Faulkner had crept up the wall of the building. The men had opened the door by overriding the failsafe and had filtered inside.

They had left it open behind them.

He could hear their voices, low and hard, as they moved farther into the ground floor.

Faulkner took out the cylindrical flash-bang and clasped it in the web between his right thumb and forefinger. He slid his left index finger into the ring pull.

"Three. Two. One. *Mark.*"

He pulled the pin, the spoon sprung up and he rolled the grenade into the darkened room beyond.

The flash-bang blared a starburst of light through the doorway.

A second flash-bang detonated a fraction of a second after the first.

Faulkner rolled around and raised the FN F2000.

He heard firing from the other side of the room. He saw muzzle flash, neat and regular, every three seconds.

Aim and shoot.

Aim and shoot.

Aim and shoot.

The Sig fired out: *blam, blam, blam.*

Rose was good.

Every shot found its mark.

Better than good. She was *unbelievably* good.

She stopped firing, ducked back to reload.

There were two Manage Risk guards nearer to him than to her. They were still stunned, just turning in the direction of the sound of Rose's gun, their backs to him. He pressed the bullpup into his shoulder, squeezed off a controlled burst, aimed again, squeezed off another burst.

The first man went down.

The second man went down.

He ducked back into cover to allow Rose to fire. She did, and the final operative hit the deck.

"Clear," Rose shouted, no need for the radio now.

"Clear," he confirmed.

"Let's get moving."

Rose changed magazines as they hurried out into the hot night. The Freelander was parked around the block. Faulkner reached it and turned. They were lagging behind him. West must have been struggling.

And then he realised: it wasn't West.

It was Rose. She was moving awkwardly.

"Are you hurt?"

"I'm fine," she said irritably. "Start the car. We're taking too long."

Chapter Thirty-One

They drove back to the foundry.

Mackenzie West sat in the back.

"Who are you?" he asked finally.

"Friends."

"Sent by who?"

Faulkner turned in the seat to look back at him. "You have something you want to say about what happened the other day, don't you? The riot?"

"Yes, sir. I do."

"We're going to make sure you get the chance to say it."

"Who sent you?"

"That doesn't matter."

"Not the government."

"Not *your* government, Mr West. I think they'd rather you were quiet, don't you?"

"I don't care what they think."

"That's the spirit."

"You're getting me out of the country?"

"Yes," Beatrix intervened. "We're just picking up some friends first."

They had left Faik and Mysha in a twenty-four-hour café attached to a gas station on the edge of town. They had dropped them there earlier, and after two short jabs of the horn, they emerged. They looked frightened and vulnerable. Beatrix felt a catch in her heart as she watched the girl reach out for her brother's hand and lead him across to them.

Beatrix got out. "Are you alright?" she asked when they had reached them.

"We are fine," Mysha answered for her brother.

"Who is that?" Faik asked, pointing at West.

"His name is Mackenzie. I was sent here to bring him out of the country."

"Why?"

"He worked for the contractors."

Faik's face flashed with anger as black as his bruises. "Then what is he . . ."

"He's going to give evidence against them. He was there when your mother was shot. He wants justice for her. For her and all the others."

The lights of a car that Beatrix didn't recognise swept into the sandy lot.

"Who is that?" Faik said fretfully.

Beatrix turned to Faulkner. "Pope?"

"I think so."

"You *think*?"

"Who is it?" Faik repeated.

"It's your ride out of Iraq," she said. "It's fine. We're here. We'll make sure you get away safely. Stay here, alright? I'll be back."

She turned to Faulkner and indicated with her eyes that he should stay with them. He nodded his understanding.

She stepped up to the car. It was a Toyota Camry, slathered in dust. The headlights burrowed into the darkness and made it difficult for her to see any details beyond a black silhouette.

The door opened, and a man stepped out.

"Turn the lights off."

The man bent down and killed the lights.

"Hands where I can see them," she called out.

"Easy!"

She raised the pistol and aimed. "Hands up, right now."

The man did as he was told.

He stepped forward so that she could see him.

"Easy. It's me."

It was Pope.

"You think maybe you might have told me that you were going to come out here, too?"

"I wasn't planning on it. I didn't think you'd be planning something as stupid as a jail break."

She glowered at him.

He indicated the al-Kaysis. "These the two?"

"Yes."

"And West?"

"In the car."

"Duffy?"

"Yes," she said.

He took another step forward and squinted at her. "Are you alright?"

"What do you mean?"

"You look dreadful."

"It's been a long day," she said, waving his concern off.

"Beatrix . . ."

"I'm fine," she said sharply. "Get back in the car. You need to get them out of here."

"Has he given you anything about Control?"

"No," she said. "Not yet. Please, Pope. Get going. You don't have time to wait."

Pope walked to the Toyota and got back inside.

Beatrix went to the Freelander and opened the rear door.

"That's your ride south," she said to them all, but she was looking at Mysha.

West and Faulkner got out.

"Thank you," Mysha said. "Again."

"Hurry," Beatrix said. "You need to get going."

The girl slid out of the car.

"Look after her," Beatrix told Faik.

"I will."

"You'll be alright."

"I know," he said. He offered her his hand, and she took it. "Thank you."

"Go."

Mysha came around the car and fell into her arms for the second time that day. Beatrix hugged her close, her face buried in her neck, and for just a moment, she thought she could smell the scent of Isabella's hair. Her heart felt swollen and her eyes stung. She disentangled herself, stood and laid a hand on the girl's cheek.

"Good luck, Mysha."

The girl smiled up at her through a curtain of grateful tears. Beatrix withdrew her hand, smiled a sad smile back at her and turned away.

Chapter Thirty-Two

Beatrix sat in the back, and Faulkner drove them farther out into the desert. They followed Pope for a few miles before reaching a turn in the road and branching away from them. She watched the red glow of the tail lights in the darkness of the early morning, fainter and fainter as the cars sped away from one another. Beatrix thought of Faik and Mysha in the back of the car. They would be safe now. Pope would get them over the border and deliver them to their family. She had done all she could for them.

She took out the burner phone and called the Manage Risk facility at Energy City. She explained to the operator that Mrs Sascha Duffy, the wife of Bryan Duffy, could be found locked in the walk-in refrigerator in the canteen of a foundry on the edge of town. She gave the woman the exact location, made her recite it back to her and then ended the call. She ejected the micro-sim, snapped it in two, and then tossed it and the phone out of the window.

Faulkner was quiet, his attention on the road.

Beatrix sat quietly, too, thinking about her list and what she still needed to do.

The cough, when it came, took her by surprise. It started as a tickle in her throat and then worsened, a whooping bark that took thirty seconds to subside.

Faulkner slowed the car.

Beatrix waved him off, and after examining her in the mirror, he gently accelerated again.

"Jesus," he said. "What was that?"

"Sand in my lungs. I'm fine."

"If you say so." They picked up the speed that they had lost.

"Where do you want to take him?" he asked.

"Keep going. Somewhere no one will see us."

She stared out the window. She concentrated on her breathing, keeping it even, focussing on it, trying to detect anything that was out of the ordinary. Any new symptoms.

The terrain dipped down between sand dunes, and the lights of Pope's car winked in and out and then finally they disappeared.

They drove for an hour. It was two in the morning when they eventually arrived at a wide-open stretch of desert that offered views of the road in both directions for several miles. There would be no chance of anything coming across them unexpectedly.

"Here," Beatrix said.

Faulkner slowed and drew up to a halt on the margin of the road.

He took the FN F2000 from the passenger seat, stepped out and opened the back. Duffy was crammed into the compartment, his feet resting on one of the wheel arches. Beatrix prodded him with the Sig, and he rolled out, stumbling a little as he did. She took her knife and sliced through the tape around his ankles. She pushed him into motion, setting him off into the dunes.

The three of them walked for five minutes until they were about two hundred yards from the Freelander.

They stumbled down into a shallow depression, the sand rippling down after them.

"Far enough," she said.

He stopped.

She pulled the hessian sack over his head, tore the tape from his mouth and pulled out the rag that was stuffed inside.

He gasped.

"On your knees," she said.

"Rose. Let's talk about this."

"On your knees."

"Come on, Rose. I didn't do anything."

"Really?"

"I was there, sure, but . . ."

"You're all culpable."

"Control said you'd gone over to the other side. He said we had to bring you in and search your place. That's it. What happened when we got there . . . fuck, I swear, I had no idea that was going to go down. It's Chisholm. She was in charge. It's . . ."

"I don't really care, Duffy. It doesn't make any difference to me what you say. You and the others ended my life. You killed my husband. You made sure I missed my daughter growing up. Instead of happy memories, all I have is bitterness and anger. What do you expect me to do? Give you a free pass? That's right, Duffy, it was all a great big misunderstanding. Right? You were just following orders."

"I was Number Eleven. I was green. I didn't know the first thing about the Group, and I didn't know what Control was planning to do."

"So we should just let bygones be bygones. That's right, yes?"

"I don't expect you to . . ."

She struck him across the face with the barrel of the pistol. *"Shut up."*

He hung his head, and, when he looked back up at her again, there was fresh blood soaked into his wild beard.

"You have one chance, Duffy. You and the others, you've all got a price to pay, and you're going to pay it, but it's Control I want. You tell me where I can find him, and I'll make it quick and painless for you."

"That's not an appealing deal."

"It's the only one you've got."

He squinted up at her. "He's with us."

"With Manage Risk?"

"Yes."

"Where?"

"North Carolina. There's a complex there."

Beatrix knew all about Manage Risk's American training facility. The company was headquartered there, and all of its staff passed through its proving grounds. "What does he do?"

"He's on the board. Him and Jamie King, back in the day, they practically set the company up. Someone like him, with his contacts, can you imagine how valuable that is? No one's ever asked how it grew so fast. That's how. He had so much intelligence, before anyone else, and amazing contacts. He could pitch for business before the companies and the governments even knew they had a need for it. And look at it now. A multi-million dollar company."

Beatrix felt the cough coming again. "How did you get involved?"

"When it was obvious that you'd found out what he'd been up to with the Russians, Control got spooked. He cleaned house and went straight to Carolina. Me and the other five all got reassigned out of the Group, and then, after a few months, he had us all meet him in New York and told us he had an idea. He was working with King, full-time, doing it properly, and he said we should work with him, too. We all said yes. Joyce worked in the nautical department. I came out to this hellhole."

"What about English? Where's he?"

"Coming after you. Control sent him here. He might be here already."

Beatrix coughed. Three hacking rasps that subsided just as soon as they started. Faulkner looked across at her. "How much does he know about me?" she asked when she had recovered.

Duffy looked back at her with a new curiosity. "He knows about what you did to the three of them, to Spenser, Joyce and Chisholm. He knows you're coming."

"Get on your knees," she said, but then she suddenly found herself short of breath. There was no cough this time, no tickle in the throat. It was a gasping emptiness that came on quickly, with no warning, and she felt the compulsion to breathe more quickly to compensate.

She started to choke.

Duffy didn't kneel.

He looked at her with a glimmer of feral cunning.

A wolf smelling weakness.

"Are you alright?" Faulkner asked.

"Knees . . ."

It felt like she had liquid in her lungs. She tried to cough, but it didn't help.

Faulkner took a step toward her. "Beatrix?"

She took a step back.

She didn't want sympathy.

She didn't need help.

Her arm dipped, her aim dropping from Duffy's head to his chest.

Not now.

I have too much still to do.

She raised her arm again. It was a struggle.

"Come on, Rose!" Duffy protested. "I told you what you wanted to know." They were just words, meaningless, ways to spin the time out as he assessed his odds.

She coughed again, wheezing, assailed now by a battering wave of fatigue. The gun felt very heavy in her hands. She had the urge to put it down, to just lay it on the ground.

Please.

Not now.

Just three more.

I'm only halfway done.

Faulkner put a hand on her shoulder. "Beatrix?"

Beatrix and Faulkner had both taken their eyes off Duffy for a moment.

A moment was all he needed.

He kicked down with his right foot and sent a spray of sand into their faces.

Beatrix was blinded, and as she raised her hands to her burning eyes, she dropped the Sig.

Duffy roared as he stretched his arms, hard enough to pop tendons as he stepped his feet over his wrists.

He burst out, barrelling into Faulkner and shoulder-charging him to the ground. He forced the assault rifle away to the side, and when Faulkner fired off a round, the bullets scattered harmlessly into the air. Duffy was big and fuelled by desperation, and Faulkner was blinded and had been taken by surprise. He squinted through the grit in his eyes as Duffy pinned his right arm beneath his right knee and then forced his left into a similarly constrained position. He prised the FN F2000 from Faulkner's fingers, reversed it and used the stock to bludgeon him about the head. He grasped it between both taped hands, driving down into Faulkner's face with all of his considerable strength.

One.

Two.

Three.

He looked demonic.

Faulkner stopped struggling after the third blow.

His body spasmed, his leg twitching.

Beatrix threw herself at Duffy, knocking him off Faulkner's body and driving him into the desert. The FN F2000 fell and was kicked away as they struggled. He rolled as they hit the ground, both of them wrestling to be on top. Duffy was twice Beatrix's weight, and she was already weak from coughing. He rolled again, forcing her beneath him. They had fallen near her discarded pistol, and he reached for it, his fingertips brushing the muzzle and then fixing around it as he stretched out. Beatrix elbowed him in the face, but he absorbed the blow, moulding the grip into the palm of his right hand and slipping his index finger through the trigger guard.

There was no safety on the Sig; it just needed a firm squeeze of the trigger to shoot.

Beatrix wrapped the fingers of her right hand around his wrists and tried to keep the gun pointed away, but Duffy was heavier, stronger, and he had leverage on her. The taped hands were to his advantage now. He could use both arms.

He pushed the gun down on her until the muzzle was jammed up against her throat. Blood ran from his nose onto his beard and dripped onto Beatrix's face.

He leered down at her. His eyes bulged with hatred.

Beatrix's left hand broke away and swept across the desert floor.

"Want to know something?" Duffy said, grunting with the effort of holding her down.

Her questing fingers felt something, fastened around it.

"We all knew what we were doing that day. We were in on it. You had it coming to you, you sanctimonious . . ."

Beatrix crashed the rock in her left hand up against the right side of Duffy's head.

A moment of stunned surprise replaced the loathing, and then that, too, winked out. His features slackened, and his eyes rolled up into his head.

He dropped onto her.

Beatrix shoved him aside and scrambled clear.

She hurried to Faulkner. He was unmoving. She took his chin in her hand and turned his head so that she could look into his face. It was a bloody mess, his eyes puffed over and glassy.

She searched for a pulse.

Pointless.

There was a groan and then the sound of scrabbling away to her right.

"You . . . fucking . . . bitch."

Duffy was on one knee, forcing himself upright, the pistol aimed at her.

He fired twice, both rounds missing by a solid yard.

Rose pulled out a throwing knife and, in the same motion, sent it spinning towards him.

The blade thudded into his right eye, and he jack-knifed from the waist, bent backwards with his arms splayed out as if he were embracing the moon.

He spasmed and then was still.

Beatrix fell to her knees. The enervating wave of lethargy rose up again, subsuming her, and she had to brace herself with both hands.

She coughed hard, a hacking rattle, and when she spat the phlegm out, it stained the sand with ribbons of blood.

She pressed down and got to her feet. She put one foot in front of the other, her boots disappearing into the loose sand, and slowly and methodically made her way back to the road.

Chapter Thirty-Three

She could have exfiltrated by retracing her way in with Faulkner, driving south across the border to Kuwait and then flying out from there. That route would mean she would be less likely to be detected and it would be much safer, but she was weak. She was frightened of how feeble she felt, and the prospect of that long drive was so daunting that she was not prepared to consider it. There were other options. She could find her way to Baghdad and fly out, or she could gamble and depart from Basra. In the end, ease won out. Basra was closest. She knew it was a risk, but it was one that she was prepared to take.

Because there were other benefits in that risk, too.

She was ready to lay some bait.

That was not to say that she was blasé about the dangers. She returned to the tailor's shop and asked him to collect the things that she would need. He had a small flat above his shop, and he showed her up to it and told her she was welcome to stay for as long as she wanted. There was a tiny bathroom adjacent to the bedroom, and she stripped off and showered, washing the sand and the grime from her skin. That helped. She scrubbed her hair and hung her head, watching as the dirty water drained away.

She turned off the water, wrapped herself in a towel and got out. She sat down on the bed and took a moment. She was finding it difficult to breathe. She knew that dyspnea was a symptom of the cancer, one of the symptoms that was most usually suffered as the disease reached its conclusion. It felt as if she had liquid in her lungs that she couldn't clear. She knew that there were medicines that would help alleviate it, but she would have to wait until she was back in Marrakech to see about that.

She took two Zomorph tablets, slugging them down with a glass of tepid water, and lay back on the bed for a moment. She had intended to wait there only until the shortness of breath was under control, but she slept as soon as she closed her eyes.

When she opened them again, it was dark outside.

The tailor must have heard her stir. He knocked softly on the door and brought her the things that she had requested. There was a small carry-on suitcase with a change of clothes inside. There was an envelope with a fake passport and a ticket to Casablanca.

"Is there anything else you need?"

"A taxi."

"It's alright. I will drive you."

"Thanks."

"Mr Pope has contacted me. He wants to know that you are alright."

"I'm fine," she said. "Did you tell him about Number Twelve?"

"Yes."

"What did he say?"

"He hopes that you are alright."

She nodded, the fatigue buffeting her again.

"*Are* you alright?" he asked.

"I'm just tired," she said. "I need to get home."

The tailor left her alone again. She listened to the noises of the city outside the window: car horns, engines, a jet streaking across the sky. It was busy, and yet she felt utterly alone.

She took out her cellphone and dialled the only number that she carried in her memory.

Mohammed's voice sounded very far away. "Hello?"

"It's me."

"It is good to hear your voice." Like her, he was careful not to use names on an unshielded line. "How are you?"

"It's done."

"Very good. And you?"

"Tired. Very, very tired."

"Where are you?"

"In theatre."

"You can get out?"

"Yes," she said. "Don't worry."

"Would you like to speak to your daughter?"

"Yes."

There was a pause, a quick conversation conducted sotto voce, and then Isabella's voice.

"Mummy?"

Beatrix felt a surge of emotion, and for a moment, her throat felt tight and choked.

"Mummy?"

"Hello, sweetheart."

"Are you alright?"

"Yes. I'm fine."

"I've been practising on the range. I'm getting better all the time."

She winced, more remorse. "That's good," she said, substituting enthusiasm for the regret she felt.

"When are you coming home?"

"Today."

"I've missed you, Mummy."

"And I've missed you, sweetheart. I've missed you very, very much."

"It's nearly done though, isn't it?"

"Nearly done," she said, noticing that her hand was gripped tight around the phone. "Two more and that's it."

Connor English sat at the row of leather chairs in the departures lounge at Basra International and watched with a mixture of disbelief, wariness and elation as the woman he clearly recognised as Beatrix Rose went by. He had a picture of her from a decade ago on his phone, and he looked down to double-check that he was right. She had been younger then, obviously, but there was no mistaking the sharp cheekbones and the cobalt-blue eyes. She was wheeling a small suitcase behind her and had no other possessions with her apart from her boarding card, a bottle of water and a copy of the *Chicago Tribune*.

The disbelief was because he couldn't believe she would have been so reckless as to exfil from out of an airport.

The wariness was because he knew exactly what she was capable of doing.

The elation was because now, maybe, he would be able to put an end to the threat that had been dogging his sleep ever since Oliver Spenser had been gunned down outside the *dacha* in the Russian steppes. Four down already and just two more to go. Him and Control.

Perhaps now he could put an end to the fear that he wouldn't wake up or, if he did, that it would be with one of her knives pressed against his throat.

Because English had been in her house that afternoon almost a decade ago. He had been Number Nine then. He knew that his name was on the list she was methodically working through. He had not expected to be in a position where he might have the advantage of surprise over her. That was the prerogative of the hunter, not the hunted.

Now, though?

Now, he would.

He got up and followed her as she walked to her gate. She moved gingerly, as if in pain, although there was nothing visibly wrong with her, and when she stopped to gather her breath, he caught the reflection of her face in the window of a book store. She was grimacing in discomfort.

She continued on to Gate Fifteen and took a seat where she could look out at the passengers circulating around the terminal. Inherent caution, tough to shake. English walked by, pretending to compare the information on his boarding card with the flight details displayed above the gate. He moved on another two gates and took a seat where he could keep an eye on her. He wanted to be sure that she got on the plane.

He took out his encrypted phone and dialled.

"Yes?"

"It's me. I have her."

"Where?" Control pressed impatiently.

"Basra. She's at the airport."

"What?"

"I know. I couldn't believe it either."

"What is she *doing?*"

"Your guess is as good as mine, sir. But she looks like she's been through the mill. Moving very gingerly. Looks like she's in pain."

"Maybe Duffy . . ."

"Maybe," English finished for him. Duffy was nowhere to be found, and Beatrix was in town. Joining those dots didn't look too good for him, but maybe Control was right: maybe he had gone down swinging.

"Why would she leave from the airport? Surely she'd drive south?"

"That doesn't make any sense."

"So where's she going?"

"I'm checking that." English looked up. "Hold on."

There was an announcement that Gate Fifteen was boarding. He watched as she hobbled to the desk and presented her boarding card. She disappeared into the air gate.

He got up and walked quickly to the gate to make sure that she hadn't tried to elude him, maybe trying to escape onto the runway. He looked out of the windows, and there was no sign of her.

"Casablanca, sir," he said. "She's going to Casablanca."

"Very good," Control said. "Send me the flight details. There will be someone waiting for her at the other end. Wherever she's been hiding, we'll find her now. We'll flush her out." There was a pause, and all English could hear was the static on the line. "It's nearly done," Control said finally. "Nearly over."

English looked out of the broad window to the 747 outside. Control had never been on an operation with Beatrix Rose before. He just selected the targets and sent his agents out to do his bidding.

But English had worked with her.

Just the once, a job in Shibuya, Tokyo, that had led to the elimination of six Yakuza gangsters. He remembered it vividly, in living colour. He remembered the hostess bar and the six tattooed men and Beatrix Rose, her knives and her bullets, and the damage she had wrought.

A storm of blood.

Connor English knew, better than most, what she was capable of doing.

He was a soldier, an assassin, but Beatrix was of another magnitude.

He wasn't afraid to admit it: the thought of going after her kept him up at nights.

But that was what he was going to have to do.

An extract from the concluding novel in the Beatrix Rose trilogy, *BLOOD AND ROSES*

Beatrix Rose's story concludes with *Blood and Roses*. For launch information (plus a FREE novel and John Milton bonus material), sign up for Mark's mailing list. You'll find details at the end of this exclusive extract.

Here's an exclusive extract from the first chapter:

Connor English sat in the open doorway of Falcon One, his legs hanging outside the cabin. He was wearing night vision goggles, and the arid and desolate desert below was washed with a ghostly green, the scrubby trees and lonely hamlets passing beneath the hull as the chopper maintained a steady pace of a hundred knots. The pilot hugged the contours of the landscape, the chopper's altitude never rising above fifty feet, keeping it beneath the line of the hills.

The pilot came over the troop net. "Falcon One to Zero. We just crossed the border. Now entering Morocco. Morocco comms, no chatter."

"Zero to Falcon One," responded mission control at the Lodge in North Carolina. "Copy that. Green to proceed."

Everything was unfolding as they had planned: they had evaded Moroccan radar coming in, and now they had a clear run to the target. English leaned forward a little, the hot wind tugging greedily at the desert scarf he wore around his neck, and looked aft. He had a good visual of the trailing helicopter, Falcon Two. It was a hundred yards to starboard, maintaining the same careful altitude, head down and tail up, racing though the night.

Both birds were painted black and carried no markings or running lights. The two Black Hawks had been modified at the Manage Risk shop at the Lodge so that their radar cross-sections were minimised. Stealth panels, similar to those used on the B-2 Spirits, had been fitted. The rotors had been modified with decibel mufflers. There were engine shields, a retractable undercarriage and refuelling probe, rotor covers, an extra rotor blade and a totally redesigned and enclosed tail boom. The Navy had done something similar with the birds that had been used on the mission to take out bin Laden, but one of those had crashed. The Pakistanis had sold the wreckage to an anonymous subsidiary of Manage Risk for twenty million, and then they had taken the basic modifications and perfected them. The cost was significant, but they would sell it back to the government eventually, and in the meantime, their efforts were going to prove very useful.

Especially tonight.

The price of all the extra work was that they flew more slowly than a standard MH-60 and packed less punch, but they had excellent radar defeat. English had been with the rest of the team when the hangar had been opened to the North Carolina sunlight and the birds revealed. The R&D guy responsible for the program admitted that he had been tempted to kill it more than once and that although the birds had been tested, they had never been tested with a full load inside them, and had certainly never been tested on something like this.

This illicit trip into Moroccan airspace was their maiden outing.

The men inside the Stealth Hawk bore no identification.

The helos and their complement of twenty-four were anonymous.

Deniable.

Unsanctioned.

Criminal, even, when you came down to it.

If anything went wrong, if the birds crashed or were shot down, if they compromised the mission in any way, they would be on their own.

English scanned the hills and valleys, looking for landmarks that he might recognise. He had studied the satellite intel that they had bought from the CIA. That had been helpful, but not nearly as profitable as the week that he had spent in the city itself. He had taken advantage of that time to acclimatise himself to the target and the surrounding neighbourhood. They had considered several ways of achieving the mission objective. They could have assaulted the riad from the ground, but it was buried deep within the medina, with very poor access. Some of the alleyways that they would need to negotiate were barely wide enough for travel in single file; this was especially true for the big men in the chopper with their hefty packs. The alleys were potential choke points, and that made English nervous.

So he had proposed this alternative.

They would fly in.

The initial plan had been to take the target out when she was outside the riad, but in the time that English had spent in the city he hadn't seen her once. She was holed up. That wasn't really a surprise. She had received the same training as he had, and she would have known, without question, that what she had already done demanded a response.

Oliver Spenser.

Joshua Joyce.

Lydia Chisholm.

Bryan Duffy.

The four of them had been assassinated, and they hadn't managed to lay a glove on her.

She had a list, and there could only be another two names on it.

Himself.

And Control.

They had to strike first.

The roar of the chopper's twin General Electric T700 turboshaft engines filled the cabin. Little else was audible beyond that and the beating of the rotors. He leaned back and pressed the wax plugs deeper into his ears. He could just make out the shape of the crew chief holding up five fingers.

Five minutes.

To continue this extract (and to get a free bestselling novel), sign up to Mark's mailing list at http://eepurl.com/VTeub

Acknowledgements

I am indebted to the following for their help, all above and beyond the call of duty: Lucy Dawson, for her early edits and direction; Martha Hayes, for masterful and thoughtful editing; and Detective Lieutenant (Ret'd) Edward L. Dvorak, Los Angeles County Sheriff's Department and Joe D. Gillespie, for their advice on weapons and military matters.

The following members of Team Milton were also invaluable: Lee Robertson, Nigel Foster, Frank Wells. Gary Pugsley, Brian Ellis, Bob, Mel Murray, Phil Powell, Charlie, Matt Ballard, Edward Short, Desiree Brown, Don Lehman, Barry Franklin, Corne van der Merwe, Dawn Taybron, Paul Quish, Carl Hinds, Chuck Harkins, Don, Bernard Carlington, Julian Annells, Charles Rolfe, Michael Conway, Grant Brown, Rick Lowe, Randall Masteller, Steve Devoir, Chris Orrick, Mike Stephens, Rick Seymour, Pat Kirk, Dale McDonald, Robert Lass, Bill Dawson, Rob Carr, Ian Clarke, Chris Goodson, Jared Gerstein, Roman Pyndiura, Cecelia Blewett, David Schensted, Caleb Burton, Louis Pascolini, Sonny de Castro, John Hall, Matt Bawden, JKP, Richard Stewart, Bev Birkin, Dave Zucker, Steve Carter, Christian Bunyan, Daniel Caupel, Debra Koltveit, George Wood and Linda French.

About the Author

Mark Dawson has worked as a lawyer and in the London film industry.

He has written three series: John Milton features a disgruntled government hit man trying to right wrongs in order to make amends for the things he's done; Beatrix Rose traces the headlong fight for justice of a wronged mother and trained assassin; and Soho Noir is set in the West End of London between 1940 and 1970. Mark lives in Wiltshire, in the UK, with his family.

You can find him at www.markjdawson.com, www.facebook.com/markdawsonauthor and on Twitter at @pbackwriter.

Printed in Great Britain
by Amazon

21038854R00130